grabbed some of her dad's coconut cakes and worked the line, selling them. Mom had to give Emma a shopping bag to hold the donations because the box just wasn't big enough.

"This is amazing," I told Dad as we watched Brady sign another autograph and watched another bill go into the donation bag.

Dad nodded. "Devin, I honestly think you might have made enough money today to get the program started," he said. "If we can find another volunteer coach to help out, I'm sure the school board will give us the go-ahead."

"Really?" I asked.

Dad nodded. "You did it, kid. Another goal scored for Devin. How'd your other two go?"

"Great," I said. "Looks like I made my hat trick!"

"That's my girl," Dad said, ruffling my hair.

I was pretty sure that Brady would have signed autographs all night, but we had to leave the community center by four, so Dad had a good excuse to kick everyone out. Then a limo pulled up and the crowd followed Brady outside as he got in.

"Thank you so much," I said. "You helped save the soccer league! You're going to make a lot of kids happy."

"That's what I do," Brady said.

Then Emma pushed her way through the crowd. "Brady! Don't forget me!" she called out.

"Emma, believe me, you are unforgettable!" Brady said, and then the limo pulled away.

Emma looked like she might faint. "Did you hear that? Unforgettable! He called me unforgettable!"

With Brady gone, the crowds quickly cleared out. We helped clean everything up. Pretty soon it was just me, Jessi, Emma, Zoe, and Frida left. My parents and Jessi's parents waited in the parking lot to take us home.

Maisie ran up to me. "Devin, you're the best sister!" she said, hugging me. "All of you are the best!"

I had to admit, at that moment I thought Maisie was the best sister too. But I would never tell her that. It would go right to her head.

"Maisie!" Mom called, and then Maisie went running off to join her.

I looked at my friends.

"Frida, thanks for bringing Brady," I said. "You totally saved the fair."

Frida shook her head. "No way. You guys worked so hard on this. You did it."

"We all did it," said Jessi. "You know why?"

We all knew the answer.

"Because we're the Kicks!" we cried.

And right then I knew there was a better feeling than scoring a goal. Or even completing a flawless hat trick.

The best feeling of all is that feeling you get when you're with your friends and everything is awesome and nothing else in the world matters. And I knew, down to my mismatched socks, that as long as I had the Kicks, I would always, always have that feeling.

ALEX MORGAN

Simon & Schuster Books for Young Readers
New York   London   Toronto   Sydney   New Delhi

Also in Alex Morgan's The Kicks series

Saving the Team
Sabotage Season
Win or Lose

SIMON & SCHUSTER BOOKS FOR YOUNG READERS
An imprint of Simon & Schuster Children's Publishing Division
1230 Avenue of the Americas, New York, New York 10020
This book is a work of fiction. Any references to historical events, real people,
or real places are used fictitiously. Other names, characters, places, and events
are products of the author's imagination, and any resemblance to actual events
or places or persons, living or dead, is entirely coincidental.
Copyright © 2015 by Alex Morgan
All rights reserved, including the right of reproduction in whole or in part in any form.
SIMON & SCHUSTER BOOKS FOR YOUNG READERS is a trademark of Simon & Schuster, Inc.
For information about special discounts for bulk purchases, please contact Simon & Schuster
Special Sales at 1-866-506-1949 or business@simonandschuster.com.
The Simon & Schuster Speakers Bureau can bring authors to your live event. For more
information or to book an event, contact the Simon & Schuster Speakers Bureau at
1-866-248-3049 or visit our website at www.simonspeakers.com.
Book design by Krista Vossen
The text for this book is set in Berling.
Manufactured in the United States of America
0515 FFG
2 4 6 8 10 9 7 5 3 1
Library of Congress Cataloging-in-Publication Data
Morgan, Alex (Alexandra Patricia), 1989– author.
Hat trick / Alex Morgan. — 1st edition.
pages cm. — (The Kicks ; [4])
Summary: With the playoffs over, Devin and her seventh-grade friends decide to try out for a
soccer travel team, but friendships are threatened because not everyone makes it on to the tough,
competitive team, and in the meantime the girls are faced with a crisis—budget cuts threaten
to eliminate the soccer program at the elementary school Devin's little sister attends.
ISBN 978-1-4814-5096-6 (hardcover) — ISBN 978-1-4814-5098-0 (ebook) 1. Soccer sto-
ries. 2. Teamwork (Sports)—Juvenile fiction. 3. Friendship—Juvenile fiction. 4. Money-making
projects for children—Juvenile fiction. 5. Middle schools—Juvenile fiction. 6. Elementary
schools—Juvenile fiction. [1. Soccer—Fiction. 2. Teamwork (Sports)—Fiction. 3. Friendship—
Fiction. 4. Fund raising—Fiction. 5. Middle schools—Fiction. 6. Schools—Fiction.] I. Title. II.
Series: Morgan, Alex (Alexandra Patricia), 1989– Kicks.
PZ7.M818Hat 2015
813.6—dc23
[Fic]
2015004129

CHAPTER ONE

Steven and I went sailing across the screen of Zoe's laptop, swaying to the music.

"Ooooooooooooh, Devin," Jessi said, and poked me in the ribs.

"Ooooooooooooh, Jessi," I teased back, pointing at the computer screen as Jessi and Cody came dancing into the camera's view. Jessi and I were huddled together with Zoe and Emma on Zoe's bed, watching the video from Zoe's bat mitzvah the week before.

"Oh my gosh!" Emma shrieked. "I think it's gonna happen now!"

All of our eyes widened as we watched the screen, waiting for the moment that we hadn't been able to stop talking about all week.

Jessi and Cody glided among the other dancers, steps away from me and Steven. It was a slow song, and just as it ended, the deejay immediately launched into a fast-paced number by Brady McCoy, a new pop star who had a hit song called "Believe in Me."

As the song started, shrieking filled the air, and Emma burst through the dancers.

"This is my jam!" she yelled in the video as she jumped excitedly to the middle of the dance floor. But instead of stopping, she lost her balance.

"Whoa!" she yelled, her long, shimmering emerald-green party dress tangling up around her legs. Emma waved her arms wildly in the air for a moment, but nothing could stop her from falling. She toppled over, knocking into Jessi and Cody, who in turn bumped into me and Steven, and we all ended up in a big pile on the floor.

Zoe and Frida came running into the frame. "We'll save you!" Frida cried. But just as they reached us, Jessi and Steven untangled themselves and got to their feet, colliding with the rushing Zoe and Frida. Jessi and Steven went down again, this time with Zoe and Frida toppling too.

Lying on the bed, we all shrieked with laughter as we watched ourselves flopping around on the dance floor. In the video, Zoe was laughing so hard she had tears running down her face. We were all hysterical and went into even harder peals of laughter when Zoe's mom and my mom came up to us on the video, concerned. They tried to help us up, but we were laughing so hard, we couldn't move.

"That was so awesome!" Zoe said as we watched ourselves carrying on. "It's one of those perfect party moments you can't plan."

"Perfect party moment?" Emma asked in disbelief. "I thought I had ruined your perfect day!"

Zoe shook her head. "No way. Those are the memories I'll never forget. And I'll always start laughing when I think about the dance floor pileup!"

My own smile turned to a frown. "I wish Frida could be here with us to see it now. She would have loved it. The drama!"

"I wonder what's going on with Frida," said Jessi. Frida was our actor friend and soccer teammate on the Kentville Kangaroos. We called ourselves the Kicks, and we had just finished a pretty good season of soccer.

We all shrugged. Frida could be dramatic, and she had sent a mysterious text this Saturday morning, right before we were all supposed to meet at Zoe's house. It read: *Sorry, but something big is happening. I can't make it today. And I can't say why—yet. We'll talk soon.*

"You know Frida," Emma said, smiling. "Maybe aliens ate her homework or she had to save the world from an army of evil wizards."

Frida had started out as a nervous soccer player, until she'd figured out that if she pretended to be someone else on the field, it helped her to calm down and focus. We all helped by coming up with ideas for her. It was always a lot of fun to try to think of different parts for Frida to play.

"At least *something* exciting is happening," Jessi complained. "With the fall soccer season over and all the planning for Zoe's bat mitzvah finished, I've had too much free time on my hands. I've been so bored. I've even been looking forward to doing my homework every night."

"That is serious," I deadpanned, as Emma and Zoe burst out laughing. At one point Jessi had avoided doing her homework so much that her grades had gone down, almost getting her kicked off the Kicks! She'd turned it around and had gotten her grades way up, but we had never heard her say she looked forward to homework before.

Jessi laughed along with them. "It's true."

"I get it," I said. "I've been in serious soccer withdrawal myself." The Kicks had made it to the first game in the state championship tournament but had lost. We had come so close. I kept going over the game in my head, knowing I could have done things better. I was itching to get back onto a soccer field to put what I had learned to use. But it was only November, and the Kicks wouldn't play together as a team again until February, when practice would start back up.

Suddenly Jessi leaped off the bed. "I'm such an idiot!" she yelled, startling us all.

"What are you talking about?" Zoe asked, her eyes wide.

"The winter soccer league," Jessi said, the words coming out in a rush. "I totally forgot. And the tryouts are coming up soon. Maybe we missed them!"

"Wait. What?" I asked, my excitement growing. "There's

a soccer team we can play on until the Kicks are back together?"

Jessi reached for Zoe's laptop. "Can I?" she asked, and Zoe nodded and handed it over. Jessi began typing furiously. "You know, Devin, when you first got here, the Kicks were in bad shape. It was just for fun to play on the soccer team. I never thought about playing it seriously, which is why I never really considered the winter league. But now everything has changed!"

Jessi squinted at the computer screen. "Got it!" She clicked, and a screen came up for the Gilmore County U14 League. "Tryouts are this Monday! We haven't missed them."

"Jessi, that's awesome!" I leaped off the bed and hugged her. We began jumping around the room together.

"I'm in too." Zoe jumped up and joined us.

"And me too!" Emma sailed off the bed and collided into us like a bowling ball knocking over pins. Once again we were a pile of people on the floor. After we all managed to stop laughing and get untangled, we sat back on Zoe's bed.

"So Maisie won't be the only one in the family playing soccer this winter," I told them. "She joined her elementary school's program. Her practices start next week."

"Oh, how cute!" Emma said. "Little tiny soccer players."

I rolled my eyes. Sometimes my little sister, Maisie, could be adorable, but mostly she was just annoying. Although, I had to admit she did have some soccer skills.

I had kicked around the ball in the backyard with her the other day, and she'd showed the potential for some pretty good footwork.

Now I heard a car horn toot outside. I looked at the clock. "That must be my mom," I said. "Gotta go!"

When I walked outside, I smiled as I saw our family's familiar white van. It had traveled with us when we'd moved from Connecticut to California this past summer. Maisie called it the Marshmallow. As I climbed inside, my phone beeped, letting me know I had a text message. I figured it was Jessi, all excited about the travel team. But instead it was a text from Frida sent to all of us.

BIG NEWS! it said, followed by a bunch of emoticons of firecrackers, smiley faces, and clapping hands. *We need to video chat ASAP!*

Wow! I wondered what was going on. Before I could even tell my mom about Frida's text or the winter soccer league, Maisie let out a wail from the backseat.

"Bad news!" she yelled before bursting into tears.

CHAPTER TWO

"Maisie," my mom said, gently yet firmly. It was a voice I'd heard her use many times with my little sister. If I were being totally honest, I'd heard her use it on me too, every once in a while. But not so much lately. After all, I was in the seventh grade now. "It's okay. Take a deep breath and then tell Devin what is upsetting you."

Maisie hiccupped as she inhaled loudly. I knew she was only eight, but I thought she was getting too old for all that crying. I started to text back to Frida, but my mom put a stop to that.

"Devin, no phone right now. Maisie needs to talk to you."

Maisie nodded as I slipped my phone into my pocket. Her face was less red, and the tears had stopped pouring out of her eyes.

"The soccer program at the elementary school . . ." Her

lower lip started trembling, and I thought she was going to burst out crying again, but she didn't. "It was canceled. I'm not going to be able to play soccer."

"It was canceled? Why?" I asked, shocked. I was suddenly way more sympathetic to Maisie. If our school did away with the Kicks, I'd be crying too.

"No money," Maisie said sadly.

My mom sighed. "Budget cuts," she said, shaking her head.

"Aw, Maisie, that's too bad," I said. "Maybe they'll have enough money next year."

"I want to play now!" Maisie said, sounding on the verge of tears again.

"I know you want to play," I said gently, mimicking Mom's voice. "But I didn't know you wanted to play this bad. You used to hate getting dragged to my soccer games."

"Yeah, but when I saw you and the Kicks go to the championships, it made me want to play too," Maisie said. "Plus, I liked sending all that princess energy to Frida while she was on the field."

Frida had recruited Maisie during the championships into acting a role during a soccer match. Maisie had gotten way into it, playing along in the stands.

"Awww, Maisie, that stinks," I said as I looked into her big brown eyes. She nodded back at me sadly.

As soon as we pulled into our driveway and got out of the van, she was right by Mom's side, tugging at her sweater and asking for cookies to cheer her up. My mom was a real health-food nut, but she did keep a hidden stash of sugary and salty snacks in case of an emergency. Maisie was milking the cancellation of her soccer program for all she could.

I grabbed my phone out of my pocket and saw I had texts from Jessi, Emma, and Zoe, too. They were all meeting online to video chat at four p.m., which was only about fifteen minutes away. I texted back that I would see them soon, before I headed inside. I popped my head into the kitchen to let my parents know I'd be using the computer to talk with the Kicks.

"Hi, Devin!" Dad said cheerfully. He was at the counter, chopping up some veggies for dinner. Maisie was pouring herself a big glass of milk to have with the cookie in front of her on the table. Maisie, 1; Mom, 0. "Did you have fun at Zoe's?" he asked.

"We did. We got to see the video from the bat mitzvah and all the photos," I told him. "But Jessi had some big news. Gilmore County has a winter soccer league. Tryouts are this Monday. Can you or Mom take me?"

"Devin, that's great news!" My dad beamed. "I know you were going through some serious soccer withdrawal. And it's only been a week. I can't imagine what you would have been like waiting for the spring season to start. Probably you would have turned into a soccer zombie."

My dad put the knife he was holding down on the cutting board, put his arms out in front of him, and got a glazed look on his face. "Soccer, soccer," he moaned as he dragged himself around the kitchen, pretending to be a zombie.

I laughed while Maisie spit out a mouthful of milk. At first I thought she was laughing too, but she got all red in the face again.

"How come Devin can play soccer and I can't?" she complained.

Oh boy. I felt bad for Maisie, but I did not want to miss Frida's news, no matter what. As Dad turned to Maisie, I quickly said, "Jessi, Zoe, Emma, Frida, and I are video chatting in a few minutes. Is that okay?"

"Yes, but when I call you to dinner, you have to say good-bye and come down right away," Dad reminded me as he grabbed some paper towels. I told him thanks and then headed up the stairs to my bedroom.

I shut the door, turned on my computer, and opened up the app the Kicks used to video chat. I was the first one online, so I invited the others to join me.

Jessi came first. She had removed the usual headband from her black hair, which was now a beautiful riot of loose dreads cascading down her shoulders. She stopped chewing her gum long enough to blow a bubble, which filled the screen before it exploded onto her face. We were both cracking up as she was peeling the gum away when Emma came into the chat room. Emma's long, thick black hair was cut into bangs straight across her forehead. Since we were video chatting, you couldn't tell it at the moment, but Emma was the tallest of us all. She was the Kicks' goalie, and her height came in handy.

Zoe logged in next. She was our fashionista, with her strawberry-blond hair cut in a stylish pixie. I wore my own light brown hair in a ponytail, as usual.

I waved at them and said, "So where's Frida? And what's her big news?"

Jessi rolled her eyes. "Leave it to Frida to be late for her own video chat so she can make a dramatic entrance."

"I'm all about the drama, darling."

We heard Frida's voice right before her face popped up on the screen. She looked pretty glamorous, with her dark red hair styled in long, loose curls.

"Frida!" Emma screamed. "What's going on?"

We all started talking at once.

"Why weren't you at Zoe's?"

"What's the big news?"

"Tell us, tell us!"

"Silence!" Frida shouted over us.

She said it superdramatically, but it was effective. We all grew silent, waiting for Frida to speak. She cleared her throat, and then announced: "I got a part in a TV movie starring Brady McCoy!"

Emma shrieked so loudly that I thought my computer speakers were going to blow up. Then she dropped out of view of the camera. It looked like she fell right out of her chair!

"*The* Brady McCoy?" Jessi asked in disbelief. "The 'Believe in Me' Brady McCoy?"

Frida nodded, her eyes shining. "The one and only."

We heard Emma panting hard as she came back onto the screen, climbing back into her chair. Her bangs were a tousled mess, and she had a glazed look in her eyes. "If you are joking, so help me, Frida . . ." She trailed off.

Frida held her right hand up and twisted her middle finger over her index finger. "I swear," she said solemnly. "It's called *Mall Mania*, and it's about a group of kids who get locked in the mall overnight. There will be singing, dancing, and a crazy subplot about a group of thieves who are trying to break into a jewelry store while we're all trapped inside. We have to figure out how to stop them. I'm playing Brady's younger sister. It helps that we have the same hair color."

We all congratulated her. I had a friend who was going to be in a movie. Wow! Things like this hadn't happened when I'd lived in Connecticut.

Emma's camera once again left her face. This time she was walking around her room with her laptop, showing us all the Brady McCoy photos she had hanging up.

Her face popped back up, her brown eyes looking sad. "Why, oh why, am I not an actress? Maybe I could have been in the movie too. And my trailer could have been next to Brady's. And then one morning we'd both be leaving at the same time, and I'd trip down the trailer stairs. And Brady would come rushing over to help me, and when he helped me up and looked into my eyes, he'd fall instantly in love with me. And I'd be Emma Kim McCoy."

As she was talking, she got this faraway look in her eyes.

I laughed. "Figures you're clumsy even in your dreams!" I teased.

"She's going to be in dreamland for a while," Zoe said. "We might as well get the whole story from Frida while we wait for Emma to return to Earth."

"Right. So when does the movie start filming? Will you be in school?" Jessi asked Frida.

Frida shook her head. "I have to be on set starting this Monday. It's really exciting. They are going to have a tutor for all the kids." She frowned for a second. "This is a dream come true, but I will miss you guys."

"Shoot." Jessi sounded disappointed. "We're all going to be trying out for the winter soccer league on Monday. I guess you won't have time for that, either."

"No. I'll be filming the entire month," Frida explained. "I didn't even know there was a winter soccer league!"

"Jessi just remembered today," I told her. "It's a county league. It will give us a chance to play soccer until the school team starts up again in February."

This reminded me of Maisie's problem.

"Maisie is pretty sad," I told them. "She was all set to start playing soccer with her school's program. But it was canceled because of budget cuts." I made a sad face.

"Aw, poor Maisie," Frida said.

"Maybe we can come over and coach her or something," Emma suggested, finally coming out of her Brady fog.

"She'd like that, Emma," I said.

"Hey," Zoe chimed in. "Frida, maybe you can get Brady McCoy to play a little soccer with you on your downtime."

"I read somewhere he's a big pro soccer fan!" Emma exclaimed.

We all laughed at the thought of Frida kicking a soccer ball with Brady McCoy on a movie set.

"Can we meet him? Can we visit you on the set?" Emma asked eagerly.

Frida shrugged. "I don't know if I can have visitors or not yet. But if I can, of course!"

I wasn't Brady-crazy like Emma, but I did like his music — and thought he was really cute. I wouldn't mind getting to meet him myself. I'd never met anyone famous before!

"I can't wait to play soccer again, Frida, but it won't be the same without you," I told her.

"Does this mean we're not the Kicks anymore?" Frida asked.

"No way!" Zoe said emphatically.

"We'll always be the Kicks!" I added. "Even when we're ninety years old and in a nursing home."

"And we'll start a nursing home soccer team," Jessi joked.

I laughed, thinking of the Kicks as white-haired little old ladies kicking a soccer ball around. "We'll be state champions for our age group!"

CHAPTER THREE

Since the winter league was a county league, tryouts were not on our home field. Instead they were being held in the field by the Pinewood Rec Center. We had all been to Pinewood Park before. It was right next to Pinewood Prep School, an exclusive private school. They had a really strong soccer team, the Panthers.

Our team, the Kentville Kangaroos, had played them a few times before. In fact, one of the Panthers, Mirabelle, used to be a Kangaroo. Mirabelle had been Jessi's best friend in elementary school. She'd also turned out to be an intense player who bullied her teammates.

So when someone had been playing tricks on the Kicks, we'd blamed Mirabelle and the Panthers. It turned out we'd been wrong. The Riverdale Rams, led by a girl named Jamie, had been causing trouble for us. Mirabelle had actually helped us out.

I wouldn't exactly say that Mirabelle had become friends with the Kicks. We were more like frenemies. Which was fine, because it was definitely better to have Mirabelle as a frenemy than as an enemy!

I did a slow jog around the field to warm up, with Jessi, Zoe, and Emma keeping pace next to me. My dad had driven us all over in the van for the winter league tryouts.

"Mom had to take Maisie to Pirate Pete's Pizza Palace to cheer her up," I told them. It was one of Maisie's favorite places to go. It had arcade games and some small rides, and all the people who worked there dressed up like pirates. "Today is the day she would have started soccer practice. She was so sad."

"Aw, poor Maisie," Zoe said. "I wish we could do something to help her."

"Couldn't we, like, do a fund-raiser or something?" Emma suggested, panting slightly. "Brady McCoy did a fund-raiser concert for his local animal shelter. I watched online with the other Real McCoys. I even sent in a text donation. Boy, was my mom mad when she saw the cell phone bill. But Brady said to be generous!"

"The Real McCoys?" Jessi asked.

Emma smiled. "It's what Brady fans call themselves."

"I knew you liked him, but wow." Jessi shook her head, her dreadlocks bouncing. "That's a little overboard."

If Emma was offended, she didn't show it. "I wonder if Frida is talking to him right this very minute. Can you imagine? I would just die!" she squealed.

Emma was in the grips of total fandom. I just hoped it wouldn't interfere with her playing.

"I think a fund-raiser is a great idea," I said, trying to change the subject. "Although we'd need to earn a lot of money to get the program up and running. Maybe I can talk to my dad about it."

"I'll try to think of something too, Devin," Zoe said as we jogged.

"We've got time to think right now," Jessi teased me, "because Devin insisted on getting here so early."

"I wanted to get a feel for the field," I protested. "Since the league is county-wide, this is different. We're going to be competing with girls from different schools. We've got Pinewood and Riverdale players here today too. This will be a lot tougher than trying out for the Kicks."

Jessi nodded. "It will be tough. But the league can have as many as eight teams, so at least there is more of a chance that we'll get to play!"

"Eight teams in the league, and the county has fifteen middle schools," I said. I had looked it up. "But we're the Kicks, so of course we'll make it!"

As the field started to fill with girls, I began to doubt myself. Just a little bit. Among them were some of the toughest players we had faced last season.

But my doubt lifted when I saw some familiar faces warming up. Fellow Kicks Sarah and Anna, who were seventh graders like me and my friends, were stretching. Next to them I spotted Grace, Alandra, and Zarine, eighth graders.

We jogged over, and everyone squealed and dove in for a big group hug when they saw us.

"I'm so happy to see you guys," Sarah said as she eyed the other players on the field, who for some reason looked really big all of a sudden. "I was starting to get nervous."

"We'll do great," Grace said calmly. She always kept it together. I think that's why she made such a great co-captain of the Kicks. And the other captain? Yeah, that's me! I loved being captain of the Kicks. But now I was going to have to start from the bottom and prove myself all over again in this new winter league.

As we chatted, I heard a voice interrupt us. "Hey, Jessi."

I turned to look, and towering over all of us, even Emma, was Mirabelle. As always when she played, she wore her dark hair pulled back into a French braid. Her shiny white jersey and matching white shorts were spotless, as usual. Mirabelle always looked perfect. When I had met her for the first time when I was trying out for the Kicks, I'd quickly figured out that the flaws weren't in how she looked but in how she acted. Although we had gotten to see a softer side of Mirabelle, I wondered which side of her had shown up for tryouts today.

"I hope we get on the same team," she said to Jessi. "I'd love the chance to play together again."

I saw the surprise on Jessi's face, but she quickly adjusted it so it didn't show.

"That would be cool," she said.

"Good luck." Mirabelle nodded at all of us before jogging off.

"Wow!" Grace said. She exchanged surprised looks with Alandra and Zarine. "I'm not sure who that was, but she looked a lot like Mirabelle."

"I think being on the Panthers has changed her," Jessi suggested. "I bet it made her realize how good she had it when she was one of the Kicks!"

Mirabelle had confided in me and Jessi how competitive the Panthers were with one another. She didn't seem so happy there, but you couldn't tell it by how she played. She was still a monster on the field and made for tough competition.

As I stretched with the other Kicks, I felt a player bump into me, almost knocking me off my feet. I glanced up and saw a girl with long blond hair and cold blue eyes. It was Jamie from the Rams, the girl who'd been behind the plot to sabotage the Kicks!

"So sorry," she said, her voice dripping with sarcasm. I knew she had done it on purpose.

"Watch it," I snapped, totally thrown that she had done something like that. Although I shouldn't have been surprised. Jamie was the most competitive player I had ever come across, willing to do anything to win. I'll admit it—I like to win, but I always play fair and square on the field. I couldn't understand how Jamie thought anything other than that was okay.

I watched her walk off with some of the Riverdale

players as Jessi shouted after her, "That's right. Keep walking!" She looked at me and rolled her eyes. "That girl is unbelievable!"

None of us had time to think much about Jamie, because the tryouts were starting. We were separated into two groups to run some drills. Our group was split in half and lined up in pairs. We started with some heading and chest trapping drills. I recognized the girl across from me as a defender who played with the Panthers. She curtly nodded at me, no smile, before we started. She tossed the ball, and I focused on jumping up to meet it and putting that energy and power into the header. I headed the ball back toward her, and she caught it easily. I was proud of my control. We took turns doing that while a couple of coaches walked around, holding clipboards and taking notes.

We moved on to chest drills. I tossed the ball at my partner's chest. She caught it there, then let the ball drop to her feet and hit it back to me before it touched the ground.

She was good, but so was I. I started to relax and got lost in the flow of playing soccer. It was my favorite feeling, and I was really happy to be doing it again.

As we ran some more drills, shooting the ball back and forth to each other, one of the coaches, a tall, thin woman in a jersey and shorts, walked by, shouting out advice. "You've got to be quick, make the movement faster. If you need to take two touches, take two touches."

I felt good and warmed up as our group got divided for a scrimmage. I was on the same team as Zoe. Emma was on the other team. I saw Emma whispering excitedly to Zoe and Zoe shaking her head worriedly before the coach pulled Emma and put her in the goal.

We played in a standard three-four-three formation (three defenders, four midfielders, three forwards). Zoe and I were forwards.

One of the midfielders intercepted a pass from the other team and sent it my way. I had to run to keep up with it, but once I was on it, I kept the ball close. The defenders ran up to stop me, but luckily I had a clear shot to Zoe. I passed her the ball, and she got it and charged toward the goal and her best friend, Emma.

Emma didn't seem to be paying attention. It looked like she was staring at her gloved hand. Zoe froze, unsure what to do. In that split second a defender swooped in and kicked the ball across the field, far away from the goal.

Zoe shook her head, frustrated. She had missed a perfect scoring opportunity. The coach yelled, "Pay attention, people!"

I got another pass from a midfielder on our team, and I zipped past a defender to launch the ball into the goal. Once again I saw Emma looking like she was fiddling with something in her glove. What the heck was she doing? Definitely not paying attention to the game. The soccer ball I had launched hit her squarely in the face. She didn't even see it coming. Emma crumpled over in a heap, and

I saw her gloved hand open and her cell phone drop out onto the field.

"Emma! Are you okay?" I ran over as I heard the coach's whistle blow.

"Ouch!" She gingerly poked at her nose. "I think I'm okay. Nothing broken, anyway."

She grabbed for the cell phone next to her and picked it up. "Look!" she said excitedly. "Frida just texted me a picture of Brady McCoy!"

A cell phone on the soccer field? Emma had just completely blown her tryout!

CHAPTER FOUR

"Oh my gosh! You are kidding me! She had her phone on the field? In the goal? I've never heard of anyone doing something like that!" Kara, my best friend from Connecticut, shook her head in disbelief. We video chatted with each other almost every day, and I had been so excited to tell her what happened at today's tryouts.

I sighed. "She has gone completely Brady McCoy crazy. We knew she liked him and stuff, but ever since Frida told us she was going to be in a movie with him, Emma has gone over the edge. I don't get it. She's such an awesome goalie."

Kara wiggled her eyebrows at me. "He *is* really cute, though, don't you think?"

I giggled. "Yes, he is, but I'd never risk a soccer game over a boy!"

Kara arched an eyebrow. "Not even Steven?" she asked.

"Not even Steven," I said firmly. Like me, Steven was in the seventh grade, and he was on the boys' soccer team. In my opinion he was just as cute as Brady McCoy, and he was really nice, too. We hung out sometimes, and we had two classes together.

As Kara filled me in on what was happening back in Connecticut, I heard a strange rustling noise near my door. I saw it creak open a few inches, just enough to fit a hand through. A crumpled ball of white paper rolled in on the floor, followed by a small hand. On the back of the hand was drawn a little soccer player, the index and middle fingers acting as the legs.

The index finger pulled back and "kicked" the ball of paper into the middle of my room. "Score!" I heard Maisie's voice yell. I shook my head.

"What's going on?" Kara asked as Maisie crawled through the door, a silly smile on her face.

I usually got mad at her if she interrupted me when I was talking to Kara, but that had been really adorable.

"Come say hi to Kara," I told her. She squeezed in next to me on my chair and waved at Kara.

"Show her your soccer hand puppet," I said.

Maisie flipped her hand around and began kicking her fingers to show her creation to Kara.

"That's so cute!" Kara laughed.

Maisie pulled a sad face. "It's the only way I can play soccer."

With all the excitement of the tryouts, I had forgotten

to tell Kara about Maisie's school soccer program, so I filled her in while Maisie looked pitiful. It was a look she had perfected, and it worked with our parents. I'd hardly ever seen her make that face without it resulting in her getting a cookie, some fruit punch, or a trip to Pirate Pete's.

Turned out Kara wasn't immune either.

"Awwww, poor Maisie!" Kara squealed. She opened her arms wide. "I'm giving you hugs through the computer."

Maisie blew her kisses back, loving the attention.

I guess I wasn't immune to Maisie when she made her sad face either. *I've got to figure out a way to help her!* I thought.

The next day at lunch I sat with Zoe, Jessi, and a gloomy Emma.

"I almost took down all my Brady McCoy posters last night," Emma said sadly. "But when I looked into those beautiful brown eyes, I couldn't do it." She sighed loudly before putting her head down on the table, ignoring her cute pink bento box. Emma was Korean, and her mom was an awesome cook. She always filled the sections in Emma's lunchbox with the yummiest types of food. My mom was a health nut, so my lunch today was almond butter and jelly on spelt bread. I would have traded for Emma's lunch in a second!

"I don't get it, Emma. What were you thinking?" Jessi asked.

Emma groaned. "Frida had texted saying she would get

a picture of Brady and send it to me. It was all I could think about. It was like my brain turned to Brady mush!"

"We already know that Devin's brain is a soccer ball, and now yours is a pile of Brady mush." Jessi shook her head. "I have some weird friends."

"Hey!" I yelled, playfully slapping her arm.

Zoe, Jessi, and I laughed, but Emma still looked sad.

"There is no way I'm making the team," she mumbled, her face still on the table.

Zoe tried to reassure her. "You never know," she said softly as Jessi and I exchanged glances. Jessi and I had talked the night before. We were kind of worried for Zoe, too. She'd frozen up on that goal because of Emma, and we knew it might hurt her chances.

"They said they would post the results online today," Jessi said as she pulled her phone out of her backpack. We were allowed to use them during lunch only. "I can check to see if they are up yet. That way we'll know."

As Jessi looked, I tried to comfort Emma.

"Even if you don't make it, we'll be playing again as the Kicks before you know it." Emma was the biggest cheerleader in our group. She always saw the bright side of things, so it felt weird having to cheer her up for a change. I wouldn't have minded hearing some reassuring words myself right then. I felt I had done really well in the tryouts, but I was still anxious about knowing if I had made the winter league or not.

So when Jessi said, "It's up!" I think we all felt butterflies in our stomachs. As Jessi scrolled through her phone, she let out a whoop of excitement. "I made it! I'm on the Griffons, and so are you, Devin."

Yes! I felt like getting up and doing a little dance, I was so happy, but since we didn't know about Emma and Zoe yet, I waited.

"I don't see you, Emma," Jessi said gently.

Emma frowned, and then shrugged. "Well, we knew that was coming, didn't we?"

"How about me?" Zoe asked. I could hear the nerves in her voice.

Jessi kept scrolling. "Zoe Quinlan, Gators."

Zoe let out a big exhale. I could feel the air blow toward me, all the way across the table.

"I'm not on the same team as you guys, but at least I'll be playing." She sounded happy.

"That's great, but it's going to be weird, playing without you, and Emma, and Frida, too," I said.

"Ugh," Jessi interrupted, before Zoe or Emma could say anything. "I've got some bad news. Mirabelle is on our team, and—"

It was my turn to interrupt. "That won't be so bad, will it? She seems to have changed, and she told you she wanted to play with you."

"I'm kind of nervous about playing with her again, but I think you're right. She'll probably be a lot cooler to be on a team with this time," Jessi said. "But Mirabelle isn't the bad news. It's Jamie from the Rams. She's on our team too!"

Yikes! I thought about how she'd bumped me on purpose and for no reason at tryouts. It would be a challenge to have to play on a team with her, but I'd been through so much with the Kicks that I felt like I could handle anything at this point.

"Maybe if we're going to be on the same team, she'll cut the attitude," I said. "Soccer is all about teamwork. We're going to have to work together."

"I hope you're right," Jessi said, but then we all noticed that Emma's head was back down on the table.

"How could I have been so stupid?" she moaned. "Now you guys are all going to be playing, and I'll have nothing!"

First Maisie, now Emma. This was just so sad.

"I know!" Zoe chimed in, her eyes bright. "Emma, you are the best at cheering all of us up when we are sad. It's time for us to do the same for you. We need to have an Emma Appreciation Day!"

"I love it!" I said. "How about on Friday? There's no soccer practice, is there, Jessi?"

Jessi checked the schedule on her phone. "We've got the afternoon off to celebrate Emma."

"We could go to the mall for the afternoon," I suggested. "And go to all your favorite stores and eat at your favorite place in the food court. What do you think, Emma?"

Emma lifted her head off the table. "Can we go to the arcade, too?"

"Of course!" Jessi said.

"And Yum Yum Yogurt?" Emma asked.

"Definitely!" I laughed.

"I'm going to create an event for us on MyBook and give it the hashtag #EmmaIsExcellent," Zoe said.

Emma smiled for the first time that day. She might not be playing soccer with us for a couple of months, but no matter what, we'd always be there for one another.

CHAPTER FIVE

After school on Wednesday, Mom drove me and Jessi to my house so we could get ready and she could bring us to our first winter league practice on time. It was a bright and sunny day, 70 degrees, and I still couldn't get used to the idea that this was a "winter" league. Winter in Connecticut was gray and cold, not bright and sunny.

Jessi and I bounded upstairs to change into our practice clothes.

"I'll take the bathroom," Jessi said, and I got changed in my room.

For soccer practice I wore a T-shirt and shorts. For games the Kicks uniform was blue and white. I wondered what color the Griffon uniforms would be. A griffon was a mythical beast that was half lion and half eagle, which was pretty cool. But I would miss our kangaroo mascot just as much as I would miss wearing Kicks blue.

I sat on the bed to put on my socks. In the Kicks we all wore striped socks and did a sock swap before each game. I had a feeling that there wouldn't be any sock-swapping in the winter league, but I put on my striped socks anyway, even though it was just a practice day. They had always brought me luck.

Jessi knocked on the door. "You ready?"

"Yup!" I answered. "Let's do this!"

My right leg bounced up and down with excitement in the Marshmallow as Mom drove us to the Pinewood Rec Center. Jessi and I practically bolted out of the car as soon as Mom pulled up.

"Pick you up at six," Mom said. "Have a good practice!"

Jessi and I both thanked her, and then we jogged up to the field, toward the other girls on our team. The other players were warming up by dribbling and passing the ball. A woman with spiky dyed blond hair was standing on the sidelines, watching them with hawk-like eyes. She wore a pink, white, and blue T-shirt that said GRIFFONS on the front.

"That must be our coach," I said.

"She looks tough," remarked Jessi.

"Well, looks can be deceiving, right?" I said. "At least, I hope so."

But we learned pretty quickly that Jessi was right. At four o'clock on the dot, the coach blew a whistle.

"Line up, please!" she barked.

She had the kind of voice that got you moving. We lined up along the field and faced her.

"I'm Coach Darby," she said. "Please go down the line and tell me your name and what position you played on your school team."

Jamie from the Riverdale Rams had scored the first-place line position.

"Jamie Quinn, forward!" she said.

I listened as the other girls spoke up. There were eighteen girls on the team, but besides Jamie and Mirabelle, the only other girls I knew were Zarine and Sarah from the Kicks. I started to feel a little bit nervous. Some of the girls were taller than I was, and I'm pretty tall. What if they were all better players than I was?

Then came my turn.

"Devin Burke, forward," I said.

Jessi started to speak next to me, but Coach Darby held up her hand.

"Devin, are those regulation socks you're wearing?" she asked.

I looked down at my striped socks. I could feel my cheeks turn red.

"No, Coach," I replied.

"Well, those socks are ridiculous. White socks only for practice, and regulation socks for games. Got it?" she said.

"Yes, Coach," I said, feeling my cheeks get even redder. Luckily, that was all she had to say about my socks. She nodded for Jessi to continue.

"All right, team," Coach Darby said when everyone had finished. "Let's get warmed up."

Coach led us in some stretching exercises, and then we did some squats and push-ups. I'd been expecting that. But what she said next surprised me.

"We're going to scrimmage, nine on nine," she told us. "I want to see how you look on the field. I heard a lot of you say you played forward on your school teams. Well, the Griffons will have two forwards, and not all of you will get to play it. I need forwards who are confident on the field and not afraid of the ball."

"Two forwards?" I whispered to Jessi. On the Kicks we'd always had three. So that meant we'd have four midfielders and four on defense. With our goalie, we'd have the standard eleven players on the field each game.

"All right, count off by twos!" Coach Darby ordered.

We counted off and then split up into two teams for the scrimmage. I gave Jessi a sad little wave as she jogged off to join the opposite team.

Coach assigned us positions.

"Jamie, Devin, play forward," she said, and I felt pretty good about that. She wouldn't have let me start at forward if she didn't think I could do it, right?

That must mean she's not too mad about the socks, I reasoned, and I jogged onto the field with confidence. Mirabelle was on my team for the scrimmage, and she gave me a nod as I passed her.

"Mirabelle, take center and kick off," Coach Darby instructed, and we all took our places on the field.

Mirabelle kicked it deep into the opponent's side, and

Jamie and I ran toward the goal. Jessi got control of the ball, but Jamie shot up to her like a streak of lightning and kicked the ball away from her. I saw Jessi grab her side, like she had been hurt.

Jamie charged toward the goal but got blocked by a defender. I ran up toward her as fast as I could.

"Jamie! I'm open!" I yelled, but Jamie did a fancy move where she turned her back to the defender and dribbled the ball to the side. It looked pretty impressive, but a girl with short hair on Jessi's team swooped in and stole the ball from Jamie.

Mirabelle got the ball from her and kicked it to me. I charged down the field, my heart pounding. I had a clear shot at the goal, but I needed to get closer. Then, out of nowhere, I felt something push into my side.

I stumbled and lost control of the ball. I expected to see someone from Jessi's team—but it was Jamie!

Jamie caught up to the ball and took it to the goal. She shot it right past the goalie into the net.

I felt a wave of anger rise up inside me, and I looked at the coach. My own teammate had just pushed me and stolen the ball. That wasn't how the game was played. Hadn't Coach Darby seen what Jamie had done? But the coach was beaming.

"Nice hustle, Jamie!" she called out.

I couldn't believe how unfair that was. After we reset the ball at midfield, I was so focused on being angry with Jamie that I didn't even notice a forward from the other team whiz past me.

"Look alive, Devin!" Coach Darby barked, and I sprang into action.

I got control of the ball a few more times during the scrimmage, but I managed to score only once. If I saw Jamie was free, I'd pass it to her, because that's how teamwork is supposed to work. But Jamie took the ball away from me two more times! And besides Mirabelle, none of the other midfielders passed me the ball. They all kept trying to score goals—probably to impress the coach, I guessed.

Coach Darby blew a whistle at the end of the scrimmage. Our team had won, thanks to three goals by Jamie. Coach had us line up again.

"I saw some fearless players out there," she said. "Jamie, Kelly, Stephanie, and Sasha, you four really impressed me. The rest of you need to give me more."

I was sweating. I could feel every muscle in my body. What more did she want me to give her?

We did some basic drills for the rest of practice, and then lined up to get our uniforms—which were pink, white, and blue, just like Coach's T-shirt. After Coach dismissed us, Jessi and I walked toward the parking lot.

"What was Jamie doing out there?" Jessi asked. "You saw her elbow me, right? And I saw her keep stealing the ball from you."

"I know," I said. "Unbelievable. And even more unbelievable is that Coach Darby didn't notice."

"Maybe she did, and she doesn't care," Jessi said. "I've heard some coaches are like that. All those girls she called out were really aggressive on the field."

I sighed. "I guess I can forget about playing forward on this team. I'll be lucky if she even starts me. I can play hard, but I'm not ever going to get *that* aggressive."

Then we heard a voice behind us.

"You're good, Devin. Just keep doing what you do, and it will work out."

We turned to see Mirabelle there.

"Thanks," I said. "But I'm not so sure that it will work out."

"That's what I thought when I transferred to Pinewood," Mirabelle said. "There are a lot of strong players on that team, and a lot of girls better than me. But I didn't let that stop me. It just made me work harder."

And then she walked off.

"Is it just me, or is she getting nicer?" Jessi asked.

I nodded. "Not warm and fuzzy, but definitely nicer," I said. "Too bad we can't say the same about Jamie."

"You mean Jamie, star forward of the Gilmore Griffons?" Jessi asked, her voice full of sarcasm.

"Yes, *that* Jamie," I said with a sigh.

Then the Marshmallow pulled up, and Jessi and I climbed in.

"How'd it go?" Mom asked.

"Good," I said, but inside I wasn't so sure. In fact, I was starting to wonder if joining the winter league had been such a good idea!

CHAPTER SIX

"All right, girls, listen up," Coach Darby said at practice Thursday afternoon. "We're going to split up for another scrimmage. I saw some great aggressive playing at practice yesterday. Today I want you to direct that energy at the opposing team, not your own teammates. Got it?"

Most of the players nodded, and I looked at Jessi and raised my eyebrows.

"Does this mean it will be an easier game?" I whispered.

"Maybe," Jessi whispered back.

But of course it wasn't. Jessi and I ended up on the same team with Jamie, and Sasha and Kelly were on the other team. Jamie listened to Coach, and even though she got close to me a few times, she didn't steal the ball.

The other team, though, was brutal. Sasha was trying to get the ball from me when she accidentally kicked me in the leg! It really hurt, but I didn't want Coach to see that it bothered me, so I kept playing.

"All right, give me three laps!" Coach Darby called out when the scrimmage ended. "And I want to see you hustle!"

Jessi let out a low groan next to me as we fell in line with the other girls on the team and started to run around the track. I looked down at my calf and saw a yellow bruise forming. "These practices are inhumane," Jessi complained, running next to me.

"Well, maybe it will get better when we're all playing together against another team," I said. "We can set loose Jamie and Sasha and Kelly against our enemies."

"If they play like that in a real game, they'll be getting penalties all the time," Jessi pointed out. "And besides, what if the other teams play like that against us?"

I hadn't thought of that. "Well, I guess it's a really competitive league," I said. "We're in for a lot more bruises before the season is over."

"Yeah," Jessi said with a sigh.

Coach Darby dismissed us after our laps. Jessi and I walked toward two of the other players—Janet and Courtney.

"See you Saturday," I said, smiling. But they didn't answer me, or even smile back.

I shook my head as we passed them. "There is no teamwork on this team either," I said. "It feels familiar. Remember on the Kicks, when the eighth graders were ignoring the seventh graders?"

"This is even worse," Jessi said. "Because nobody is sticking together."

"Except us," I said.

Jessi grinned at me. "Except us."

Then I heard a familiar beep, and I took my phone out of my sports bag. It was a text from Emma.

Can't wait for the mall tomorrow!

I texted her back. *#EmmaIsExcellent.*

Emma simply replied: ☺

I gave her a ☺ right back. The Kicks might not have been a team right then, but that didn't mean we weren't still the Kicks. No matter how tough it got on the Gilmore Griffons, I still had my friends.

The next day at school seemed to go by sooooo slooooowly, because all I could think about was going to the mall with my friends. It wasn't that I was in love with the mall or anything, but I missed seeing my friends at Kicks practice every week. I knew we saw each other at school, but it wasn't the same thing.

So when the last bell rang on Friday, Jessi, Zoe, Emma, and I raced out the door to Jessi's mom's minivan.

"Wow, you guys have lots of energy," Mrs. Dukes said.

"It's Emma energy," Zoe told her. "We're celebrating Emma today."

"Oh, is it your birthday, Emma?" Jessi's mom asked.

"Nope," Emma replied cheerfully. "It's because I'm a loser!"

"Emma, that's not true," I said.

"Well, technically it is," Emma said. "And anyway, I don't mind. If I get an Atomic Burrito out of all this, then I will embrace my loserness!"

"I don't even think that's a word," I said.

"Well, it is now!" Emma said.

Then all our phones made a noise at the same time. We all checked to see a text from Frida.

Sorry I can't be there. Busy on set!

And she'd sent a picture too, of her and Brady McCoy drinking out of a soda can with two straws in it and making funny faces.

"Oh my gosh!" Emma squealed. "Look how close her lips are to his!"

"I think they're just goofing around," I said.

Emma sighed. "I wish I could goof around with Brady McCoy like that."

Mrs. Dukes dropped us off in front of the Sun Center mall. We walked through a row of palm trees to the entrance.

"Where to first?" I asked.

"Sports World!" said Jessi and Zoe.

"Cute Emporium!" said Emma at the same time.

She turned to Jessi and Zoe. "Uh-uh. No Sports World today. We're here so I can forget about not making the soccer team, remember?"

"You're right!" Zoe said, linking elbows with Emma. "Cute Emporium it is!"

I didn't go to Cute Emporium a lot, but it was like the

store had been created especially for Emma. Everything the store sold had a supercute animal face on it—big eyes and a little pink nose. Adorable faces stared out at us from mugs, notebooks, T-shirts, backpacks, and just about any other item you could think of.

Emma made a beeline for an alarm clock with a spotted fawn on it.

"Sooooo cute!" she said. "Almost as cute as Brady."

Zoe groaned. "I know this is your day, Emma, but do you think we could get through this without you mentioning Brady's name every five minutes?"

Emma looked thoughtful. "Um, no."

I would have been happier in Sports World myself, but I looked around and found a cute key chain with a puppy sitting on top of a soccer ball. It was only a few dollars, so I bought it.

"Maisie will love this," I told Jessi, holding it up to show her.

"Poor Maisie," Jessi said. "We still need to think of a fund-raiser for her soccer program."

"Maybe we could talk about it when we eat," I suggested.

"Eat? Did somebody say 'eat'?" Emma asked, looking up from a pile of plush baby seals.

"Have you had your fill of cuteness yet?" Zoe asked.

"I will never have my fill of cuteness, but right now I'm hungry," Emma said. "On to Atomic Burrito!"

We left Cute Emporium and took the escalator up to

the food court. Emma walked right to Atomic Burrito, her favorite stand in the whole place. As you might have guessed, Atomic Burrito sold burritos that were mostly on the spicy side.

Emma was the first one at the counter. "One Atomic Super Special, please. Extra spicy."

I followed her. "One Sub-Atomic Chicken, extra wimpy," I said. I hated to say the words "extra wimpy," but that was the only way you could get something to eat that wouldn't set your mouth on fire.

They made their burritos pretty fast there, so soon we were all sitting around eating our burritos and talking about Maisie's soccer program.

"It's so unfair that Maisie and her friends can't play soccer," Emma said between bites of her superspicy burrito. "I love the idea of a fund-raiser."

"Maybe a craft fair," Zoe suggested.

"Or what about a bake sale?" I suggested.

"I'd love to see us do, like, a soccer clinic for kids," Jessi said. "We could charge a small fee and donate it to Maisie's school for the soccer program."

"That would be fun," I said.

"What would be fun?"

I turned around and saw two boys standing behind me—Steven and Cody. Jessi kind of had the same relationship with Cody that I had with Steven. They liked each other, but they weren't boyfriend-girlfriend or anything. (None of our parents thought we were old enough to go out on dates, so we kept it loose.)

"Hey, sit down!" Jessi said, pulling over two orange metal chairs for the boys. I noticed Emma and Zoe look at each other and roll their eyes.

Steven and Cody were kind of opposite-looking. Cody had wavy blond hair and blue eyes, and Steven had dark eyes and short, spiky black hair. But they both loved soccer as much as Jessi and I did.

"So, how's practice going?" Steven asked.

I shook my head. "It's really tough," I said. "Coach Darby wants us all to play really aggressively, and I just don't have it in me. And nobody on the team is, like, gelling."

"Really?" asked Zoe. "It's not like that on the Gators. It's like we've always played as a team. And our coach is really nice."

"Lucky!" said Jessi.

"Yeah, the boys' winter league is really competitive," said Cody. "And the practices are a lot harder."

"I know, right!" exclaimed Jessi.

While we were talking, I noticed Emma looking down at her burrito. Her atomic smile had faded. She pushed back her chair and stood up.

"I'll meet you guys in the arcade, when you're done talking about *soccer*," she said, and then she walked away quickly before we could stop her.

"Emma, wait!" Zoe said, jumping up and running after her.

Steven looked at me. "What's that about?"

I sighed. "Emma's upset about not making a team. I guess all this soccer talk got to her. We should go after her."

"Sure," Cody said, and the two boys stood up. "See you later!"

Jessi and I looked at each other.

"Poor Emma! This must be bothering her worse than we thought," I said.

"Definitely," Jessi agreed.

We found her in the arcade, killing zombies with a laser gun while Zoe watched. I put some quarters into the machine and grabbed the laser gun next to hers.

"Behind you!" I yelled, and I destroyed a zombie that was just about to take a bite out of her arm.

Emma turned to me. "Thanks, Devin," she said, and then she smiled, and everything was all right again. The Kicks were still the Kicks.

But how long can the Kicks stick together? a little voice inside me asked. *As the season goes on, you'll be seeing less and less of Zoe and Emma.*

I pushed the thought out of my mind and blasted a zombie. I had to admit, it made me feel a lot better!

CHAPTER SEVEN

"Devin. Wake up, Devin!"

I slowly opened my eyes to see Dad hovering over me, gently shaking my shoulder.

"Dad, my alarm didn't go off yet," I told him, pulling the pillow over my face.

"It did, but you slept through it," Dad said.

A surge of panic jolted me awake. I looked at the clock: six twenty. The Griffons had a game today, and Coach Darby had called a 7:00 a.m. practice before we hit the road.

"Oh gosh, we're going to be late!" I said, jumping out of bed.

"I've got your breakfast ready, so just get dressed and you can eat in the car," Dad said.

"Thanks!" I said gratefully.

I got dressed as quickly as I could, and when I went

downstairs, Dad was waiting for me, with a thermos of coffee for him in one hand and a homemade smoothie and a granola bar for me in the other hand.

"I don't even know what Coach Darby would do if I showed up late on game day," I said. "Probably throw me off the team!"

"Is she really that tough?" Dad asked.

I nodded. "Yes. You'll find out today. You're coming to the game, right?" I asked.

Dad nodded. "Of course. I haven't missed one yet! I'm going to hang out and watch you guys practice, and then I'm driving you and Jessi," he said. "The game's at the Spring Lake field, in northern Gilmore. It's about a forty-five-minute drive."

I dragged myself out to Dad's car. Coach had called for a double practice on Saturday to prepare for our first game, and I was feeling it all over my body. We had scrimmaged again, and she'd moved me from forward to a left wing in the midfield. I wasn't happy about that, because I liked playing forward a lot more, where I had more chances to score goals. Being a midfielder was more about passing.

As we drove toward the field, I realized something. "So, wait—Mom and Maisie aren't coming to the game?"

"Well, Maisie's been so bummed out about her soccer program being canceled that Mom signed her up for gymnastics," Dad said. "She's starting this morning."

"That's good," I said. "But it stinks about her soccer program."

Dad nodded. "I know. I contacted the school and told them I'd volunteer to coach. They seemed interested, but they said they still need more funds for equipment and field maintenance."

"The Kicks and I were thinking about doing a fundraiser," I told him. "We just haven't had a chance to plan anything out, with all these practices."

"That's really sweet of you guys," Dad said. "Let me know if you need help, okay?"

"I will, Dad," I said. "Thanks!"

We arrived at the Pinewood field, and I ran out of the car. It was exactly 6:59 when I got onto the field. I breathed a sigh of relief.

"You girls are looking sleepy this morning!" Coach Darby barked at seven on the dot. "Give me thirty jumping jacks. Let's get your blood pumping!"

I looked over at Jessi. She looked just as tired as I was. Except now I was starting to get excited for the game.

"That's it, girls!" Coach Darby cheered us on. "Let's get ready to trounce those Gazelles!"

We drilled for about an hour, and then it was time to hit the road and get to Spring Lake.

"Those looked like normal drills to me," Dad said as he drove Jessi and me down the highway.

"Yeah, the drills are normal, but you should see our scrimmages," I told him.

"They're brutal," Jessi confirmed.

"Brutal how?" Dad asked.

"A lot of the girls will elbow you or trip you up to get the ball, and Coach doesn't say anything about it. And I know she sees them," I explained.

Dad frowned. "I knew this winter league was going to be more competitive. But there's a difference between being an aggressive player and being unsportsmanlike. There's no place for contact on the field."

The mood was kind of tense for the rest of the trip. I kept thinking, would the other team, the Gazelles, be elbowing and shoving? Was I ready for a game like that? I glanced at Jessi next to me, and she looked worried too.

It turned out, I shouldn't have been worried at all—not for that reason, anyway. When we got to the Spring Lake field, Coach Darby had us line up.

"Jamie, Stephanie, I want you on forward," she said. "Mirabelle, Kelly, midfield center. Janet, left wing; Meg, right wing. Katie, Lauren, Amanda, Tracey, defense. Courtney, you're on goal. Sasha, get ready to sub for Stephanie."

Jessi and I looked at each other, stunned. Had we heard right? We weren't starting? This was really disappointing, especially after all the hard work we'd put in.

On the Kicks this would have been the time when we would do a sock swap and then put our hands together for a big cheer. But the starting Griffons just jogged out onto the field and took their positions without even high-fiving one another.

Jessi and I sat on the bench with the other five team

members who weren't starting—Sasha, Beth Anne, and Kristin, and Zarine and Sarah from the Kicks.

"Devin, I can't believe they didn't start you," Zarine whispered. "You were the best player on the Kicks!"

"We're all good players," I said. "I'm sure Coach will sub us in."

But the first quarter passed with no substitutions at all. Jamie scored a goal against the Gazelles. Before the second quarter started, Coach waved to the bench.

"Sasha, in for Stephanie. Jessi, you're in for Kelly."

I high-fived Jessi as she took to the field. If I couldn't play, at least I could cheer on Jessi.

The second quarter started off with one of the Gazelles sweeping down the field and scoring a goal against the Griffons.

"Courtney, take a break!" Coach Darby called out. "Kristin, you're on goal."

Play resumed, and that was when I noticed that things started getting a little intense. One of the Gazelle defenders face-planted in the grass, and I was sure that Sasha had tripped her. Then one of the Gazelles had the ball, and I saw Jamie push her with her shoulder as she tried to get the ball!

Where is the yellow card? I wondered. If the ref had seen Jamie push another player, he would have given her a yellow card—a warning for rough play or unsportsmanlike conduct. A second warning would get Jamie out of the game.

I couldn't call for a yellow card out loud, though, because I didn't want a penalty against my own team, even if it was deserved.

Then Jessi had control of the ball, and she took it right down the center of the field.

"Go, Jessi, go!" I yelled.

Then, out of nowhere . . . *wham!* One of the Gazelles side tackled her, and Jessi fell to the ground! I couldn't believe it. I heard a ref's whistle.

"But I tripped!" the Gazelle said, but the ref wasn't buying it.

"At least there's some justice," Zarine said to me, and Sarah nodded solemnly next to her.

Right then I figured that my fears were right: Coach Darby wasn't the only coach in the winter league who expected rough play from her team.

"Jessi, you all right?" Coach Darby asked.

Jessi jumped to her feet. "I'm okay, Coach!"

There were no more scores in the second quarter, and so when halftime came, I was itching to get onto the field. My right leg was bouncing up and down like it had a mind of its own. But when Coach called out the positions, she didn't say my name, and Jessi was back on the bench.

"This is ridiculous," I complained as the third quarter began. "I want to play!"

"She's got to call you in," Jessi said.

Sasha scored in the third quarter, and we were looking good going into the fourth. But then things kind of fell apart. Jamie, Sasha, and some of the midfielders were taking long journeys down the field, not passing even when others were clearly open. The Gazelle defense kept getting the ball from us, and they managed to score twice in the first five minutes of the last quarter.

Coach Darby turned to the bench, and I thought, *This is it! She's sending me in!*

"Zarine, sub for Tracey," Coach Darby said. I waited for her to say more, but that was it.

"Sorry," Zarine said to me before she jogged out onto the field.

I wanted to melt into the bench. Not playing stank worse than dirty gym socks. And now I had my teammates feeling sorry for me too. It felt terrible—and my ego had taken a hit.

The Gazelles ended up beating us, 3–2, and everyone on the Griffons looked pretty miserable as we slapped hands with the Gazelles.

"You can do better than this, Griffons!" Coach Darby said when we came back to the sidelines.

Yeah, I know, I felt like saying. *I can do a lot better than sitting on a stupid bench!*

Then Coach dismissed us, and Dad walked up to me and Jessi.

"I see what you mean about the super-aggressive playing," Dad said.

Jessi made a face and grabbed her side. "Yeah, I'm still smarting from that tackle."

Dad didn't mention me being benched, and I was glad, because I didn't feel like talking about it. In fact, I didn't feel like talking about anything the whole ride home.

Then it hit me—when the Kicks lost, we were sad and upset, but we always bounced back. I always ended up shaking it off and laughing with my friends. But it wasn't going to work that way on the Griffons.

Soccer had suddenly stopped being fun. Soccer, my passion, the driving force of my life. Right now I didn't even feel like playing anymore.

And that was a scary thought.

CHAPTER EIGHT

Jessi and I were hanging in my room after the game, waiting for her mom to pick her up, when Zoe texted us.

How did your game go? she asked.

We lost, 3–2, I typed back.

Sorry! Zoe texted. *Gators won 3–1. Grace is on my team. I passed it to her twice and she scored!*

"What is she, giving us a play-by-play?" Jessi grumbled. I could tell she was upset about losing.

I wasn't upset, but I didn't feel like texting much either, so I replied with a 👍.

Jessi sighed. "Sorry. I'm happy for her. I just wish we could have won too."

Zoe's next text was a photo of her and some of her Gators teammates. They wore green uniforms—and mismatched striped socks! Jessi and I both noticed that detail right away.

"No way! That's our Kicks ritual!" Jessi cried.

"I guess *their* coach doesn't mind if they don't wear regulation socks," I said.

"Hey, maybe that's why we lost," Jessi said. "We didn't get to do our lucky sock swap. Maybe we're, like, cursed!"

I thought about that. I wasn't a very superstitious person, but I did always believe that somehow the sock swap brought us luck. But I knew it was more than that.

"If we're cursed, it's because we're not acting like a team," I said. "We don't even huddle before a game."

Jessi nodded. "Yeah, I guess you're right. But now I'm starting to feel like we're cursed, ending up on the Griffons!"

I almost said, *Well, at least we're still playing soccer,* but I just couldn't get the words out—because for me, it wasn't even true! I had sat on that bench the whole game!

The more I thought about it, the more being benched bothered me. Even after Jessi went home, I was still thinking about it. I thought about it during our Sunday whole wheat spaghetti dinner, and I thought about it watching the football game on TV afterward.

I had a vocabulary quiz at school the next morning, and that distracted me for a little bit. (Which is about the only good thing you can say about a vocabulary quiz, right?) Then at lunch I found another distraction—although this one was almost as bad as being benched.

Jessi and I walked into the cafeteria together, like we always did. And we walked toward our table, the one we always sat at with Zoe and Emma. The only problem was, Zoe and Emma weren't sitting at our usual table.

Jessi frowned. "That's weird. Maybe they're running late," she said as we draped our backpacks over the edges of our blue plastic seats.

But then I spotted Zoe. She was sitting at a table with Grace and Anjali—two Kicks who were now on the Gators with her. She saw me looking at her and then got up and dodged through the tray-carrying students to reach me. It reminded me of how she was on the field, weaving through other players like a little lightning bolt.

"Hey, I hope you don't mind, but I'm sitting with Grace and Anjali today," Zoe said. "We wanted to go over yesterday's game while it's still fresh in our minds."

"Sure," I said. "But you're not deserting us forever, right?"

"Of course not!" Zoe said, and then she gave me a quick hug and darted off again.

"Okay, well that explains Zoe," Jessi said. "But what about Emma?"

I scanned the lunchroom as I opened up my lunch bag, but Jessi spotted her first.

"There she is! At that corner table!" Jessi said, pointing.

"Who are those people she's sitting with?" I asked.

"Well, I'm going to find out," Jessi said, and she got up and marched off. I was pretty curious, so I followed her.

"Hey, Emma," Jessi said, and the tone in her voice said a lot more than those two words. It was a tone of voice that said, *What the heck are you doing here with these guys and not with your best friends?*

Emma stopped talking to a girl with curly hair and looked up. "Oh, gosh! I totally forgot to tell you. I joined the Tree Huggers. We meet during lunchtime."

The Tree Huggers was our school's environmental group. They were always doing stuff like making recycling posters, and they'd planted a vegetable garden on the lawn.

"Oh, cool," I said. "It's just, well, we missed you."

"You guys should join us," said the girl with curly hair. "I'm Michelle. We can always use new members."

"I'd love to, but the winter soccer league is taking up all my free time right now," I said, and I saw a shadow cross Emma's face. Then it all made sense. How could I feel bad about her joining the Tree Huggers when I was so busy with the Griffons?

"All right, so, see you later," Jessi said, and we headed back to our table. Jessi took the lid off her packed salad and started stabbing the lettuce with a fork.

"You seem mad," I said.

"Of course I'm mad!" Jessi said. "I mean, I get that we all don't have to do everything together all the time, but lunch is one thing we always do. That's our thing. It's a Kicks thing!"

"Yeah, but we're not Kicks right now," I reminded her, even though it hurt to say it.

"Yeah, I guess we're not," Jessi said, and she started stabbing at her lettuce again.

"I get it," I said. "I miss being in the Kicks. I miss Frida, too."

Jessi put down her fork. "We should text her. Maybe we could video chat during lunch."

"Good idea," I said, and I picked up my phone.

Hey Frida! How's it going on the set? We miss you!

I got a reply right away.

Miss u 2! Tutor coming back in a minute. She's no Ms. Frizzle. She'll make me do extra math problems if she sees me on the phone.

K ttyl! I replied.

"She's busy," I informed Jessi.

Jessi sighed. "Why am I not surprised?"

We pretty much finished our lunch without talking. It felt so weird, eating in silence when normally there'd be a bunch of us talking and laughing. Everything was so different now, and I didn't like any of it.

Could the winter league tear the Kicks apart?

CHAPTER nine

Dad picked Jessi and me up after school to take us to practice. We didn't run to the car like we had on the first day. In fact, we both walked extra slowly.

"I hope you two look more alive on the field today than you do right now," Dad joked.

"I don't think I'll ever look alive enough for Coach Darby," I said in my most miserable voice.

When we got to the field, I saw that my shoelace was loose. I put my foot up on the bench so I could relace my shoe and tie it.

"On the bench again, Devin?" a voice behind me asked. "I guess you really like it there."

I didn't have to turn around to know who was taunting me—it was Jamie. I could feel my face turn red, so I just ignored her. She walked off, laughing, and Jessi sidled up to me.

"Are you kidding me?" Jessi said. "You want me to say something to her?"

"Forget it," I said. "Jamie's just trying to psych me out. That's what she does. Which is a pretty stupid thing to do to someone on your own team, but that's Jamie."

Jessi just frowned, and I could tell she was really angry.

"Listen, maybe she's right," I said. "If I want to get off the bench, then I need to start playing like Coach wants me to."

Jessi raised an eyebrow. "What do you mean?"

"If Darby wants me to be more aggressive, I'll be more aggressive," I said.

"You mean, like pushing and shoving on the field?" Jessi asked.

"No. But I can be more aggressive about going after the ball. I can show Coach I really want to play and score," I said. I was not going to sit on the bench again next game. No way.

As we got in line to warm up, I saw a group of girls walking onto the field in yellow scrimmage jerseys.

"We're scrimmaging with the Giraffes today," Coach Darby announced. "Coach Perez and I are old friends, and we decided this would be a good chance to give you girls some extra practice."

Coach Perez was a tall, thin guy with a black crew cut and a friendly smile.

"He looks too nice to be Coach Darby's friend," Jessi whispered to me. I started to laugh, but then covered it up when Coach Darby marched toward us.

"Devin, Jessi, midfield center," she called out, to my surprise.

I jogged out into the midfield, grateful to get a chance to play. I knew it was only a scrimmage and didn't count toward our standings, but it felt like a real game. I knew if I had any chance of playing in our next real game, I'd have to impress Coach Darby. So at kickoff, when one of the Giraffes came dribbling down the field toward our goal, I charged toward her like a mad bull.

Normally I might have waited until she kicked the ball out in front of her, but she was keeping the ball pretty close to her as she dribbled. I could see the sweat on her forehead as I ran up to her, blocking her path to the goal. She banked to the right, and I moved with her, kicking the ball right out from under her feet. Then we both scrambled for it, but I got to it first.

Jamie was open about ten feet away from me, so I swiftly kicked it to her, and she charged toward the goal with it. My heart was pounding. I had made a successful pass! This was exactly what I loved about the game—that rush you feel when you get the ball and things work out like they're supposed to.

Coach Darby kept me in midfield for the second quarter. I tried to steal the ball from the Giraffes every time I could.

"Nice job, Devin!" Coach Darby called out, and I thought maybe she was talking to some other Devin on the field. But of course, there was only me.

Toward the end of the second quarter, one of the Giraffes dribbled the ball toward me. One of her teammates was right next to her. To get the ball I'd have to get between them.

Normally I would have gone around them, but this time I sort of squeezed my way between them, and I felt my elbow accidentally make contact with the side of one of the Giraffes. Then I heard Coach Perez's whistle blow. Play stopped, and he held up a yellow card. Then he pointed at me.

"Me?" I asked, and he nodded.

I jogged across the field to him, embarrassed. I felt like everybody was staring at me. I had never received a yellow card before.

"This is for elbowing your opponent," he told me. "One more, and you're out. Got it?"

I felt my face heat up. Of course I hadn't meant to elbow her. But it didn't matter—I had anyway. "I got it!" I promised sheepishly. And then I jogged back onto the field.

Coach Darby came toward me, and for a second I wondered if she was angry. But instead she said, "Don't let it get you down, Devin. It's okay to get a yellow card once in a while. It's a sign that you're playing to win."

A sign that you're playing to win. I wasn't sure if I agreed with that, but in that moment she honestly made me feel better. And she kept me in for the whole game!

The game ended in a tie, 2–2, and since it was just a

scrimmage, we didn't do any overtime. I was standing next to Kelly when the game ended, and I went to give her a high five, but she just rolled her eyes.

"It was a tie. Why are we celebrating?" she asked.

I couldn't believe it. How about high-fiving for a good game? Then Mirabelle walked up to me with her right palm raised.

"Up here," she said with a smile, and I slapped her palm.

"Thanks," I said. "It's hard to find anyone with team spirit around here."

Jessi ran up to us. "Tell me about it. It's really getting me down."

Mirabelle nodded. "It's kind of like how I felt when I left the Kicks to go to Pinewood," she said. "It's a really competitive atmosphere over there. I felt like a little fish in a big pond."

"Exactly," I said. "It's really hard to fit in on the Griffons."

"You did a pretty good job today," Jessi said. "Yellow card? Should we call you Bruiser now?"

"That was an accident," I protested, but as the words left my mouth, I wondered if they were true. I'd wanted to get to that ball, no matter what it took. I'd known I would have to smash my way between those two players to get it. That sounded like rough play to me.

"Well, I ended up finding my place on Pinewood," Mirabelle said. "Maybe we just all need more time to gel, you know?"

Then she glanced toward the parking lot. "See you later."

As Mirabelle left, Jessi and I looked at each other.

"I really like the new Mirabelle," I said.

"Well, people change," Jessi said, and then she looked me directly in the eyes, like she was talking about me too.

"I'm not changing!" I insisted. "I'm just trying to be a better player."

"Whatever you say, Bruiser," Jessi said, and then she laughed, and I knew she was teasing, and I laughed too. It felt like a relief.

Then my dad pulled up in the Marshmallow.

"How did it go?" he asked, and then he noticed the Giraffes. "Did you guys have a scrimmage?"

"Yeah," I replied. "We tied. I didn't score any goals, but I made some good passes."

"Great, Devin," Dad said. "It sounds like things are working out."

"I guess," I replied.

I might have been playing the way Coach wanted me to on the field, but our team hadn't won a game yet. And we never would, as long as everybody was acting like it was every player for herself.

I was determined to fix the problem. The only question was—how?

CHAPTER TEN

My problem-solving skills got a great workout the next day in school. I aced my algebra test and totally owned a surprise quiz in science. So figuring out how to fit in on the Griffons should have been a breeze, right?

My mood was pretty good when I left science class after the pop quiz. It got even better when Steven came up to me in the hall afterward. He walked over with that awesome smile of his. I know it sounds dorky, but I got this warm and fuzzy feeling whenever he smiled at me. I returned the smile, happy that my day was going so great. Usually I felt so in control on the soccer field, like I was in the flow. But I hadn't been feeling that lately, so a day of kicking butt at school helped me regain some confidence.

Then it was time for lunch, and my good mood took a hit. Emma sat with the Tree Huggers, and Zoe with her fellow Gators again. The bright side was that Jessi and

I had a lot of laughs as she showed off her new Coach Darby impersonation. Not only did Jessi nail that barking voice, but she narrowed her eyes in a perfect imitation of Coach's hawk-like stare. I laughed so hard, I almost spit coconut water (thanks, Mom!) out of my nose.

I saw Steven again seventh period, when we had World Civ together—and another quiz. When that class ended, we walked to English class. "How'd you do on the quiz?" he asked me.

"Aced it," I announced proudly.

Steven groaned. "I wish I could say the same. The last time we had a surprise quiz, it was an open book. Mr. Emmet is getting tough."

"He did say there might be a quiz on the chapter last week," I reminded him.

"A whole week ago? How am I supposed to remember that?" Steven asked.

I laughed. "There's this great invention called a notebook and a pen. You can write stuff down."

He pretended to look surprised. "What will they think of next?" he joked. "But seriously, I've been busy with the boys' winter league."

I nodded. "Yeah, the girls' winter league has been keeping me on my toes too."

"How's Emma doing?" Steven asked. "She seemed really upset at the mall."

I shook my head. "You know Emma. She doesn't stay down long. It's just been weird. Emma's not playing at all, and Zoe's on a different team." I sighed. "It's just not the same. I miss the Kicks."

"Yeah, I get it," Steven said. His smile had vanished. "My good friend Jake didn't make the league at all either. The competition was fierce at tryouts. We always used to talk about soccer. Now I don't know what to say to him. I don't want to bring it up and hurt his feelings, but avoiding it and not talking about it feels . . ." He trailed off as he tried to think of the right word.

"Like an elephant in the room!" I suggested. "It's like, no one wants to say it, but everyone knows it's there."

"That's exactly it." Steven beamed at me, smiling again. I smiled back, and I felt my cheeks getting a little red. I did mention that Steven has an awesome smile, didn't I? "So I guess we're both dealing with the same thing."

"Yeah." I nodded. "Emma is still Emma, and your friend Jake is probably the same old Jake. I guess we should just act normal around them. I mean, respect their feelings and not rub it in their faces or anything that we made the winter league and they didn't."

"And just be ourselves," Steven said. "And soon we'll be playing with them again. Man, I can't believe it, but I even miss Coach Valentine."

That really made me laugh. The boys' Kentville Kangaroos had a tough coach. He filled in once for the Kicks coach, Coach Flores, and we missed our sweet and fun coach like crazy. In the end, we'd liked and respected Coach Valentine. He was tough but fair. One thing the

Kicks couldn't decide on was whether we loved or hated his corny jokes. They were way better than all the push-ups he made us do, anyway. But we wouldn't trade Coach Flores for anyone—especially not Demolition Darby. (Yeah, I'd started calling her that in my head. Our soccer matches were starting to feel like those demolition der-bies, where cars smash into one another on purpose.)

As Steven and I walked into English class together, I felt like whistling, I was so happy. Steven was right. Soon the Kicks would be on the field together with Coach Flores at the helm. I just had to learn to deal with the Griffons and Coach Darby until then.

That night I video chatted with Kara. I had filled her in on Sunday night about my stellar job as a bench warmer at the game, so she knew all about that. I hadn't had a chance to talk to her about the scrimmage, though.

"And I tried to squeeze through instead of around the other players. Which was pretty stupid, because I ended up accidentally elbowing one of the Giraffes in the side," I told Kara. I was a little embarrassed when I said the next words: "I got my first yellow card."

"Wow!" Kara said, her eyes wide. "I mean, it sounds like you almost had to do it to get through to your coach, Devin. What did she say?"

"That's what is crazy, Kara," I said. "Coach was happy about it. I think I impressed her. It's like Jamie, Kelly, Sasha, and Stephanie are all Coach Darby's favorites. And they are the ones who play the roughest." I shook my head. "I guess it wouldn't be so bad if the Griffons were at least friendly with one another. But most of them treat their teammates like opponents too. I think that has a lot to do with why we lost our first game."

Kara let out an exasperated sigh while rolling her eyes. "What is up with that? Soccer is all about teamwork. Go play a solo sport if that's your attitude."

"I know, right?" I agreed.

"Well," Kara said. I could hear her drumming her fingers on her desk, a sign she was deep in thought. "Maybe the other girls are nervous. If they think everyone else is tough, they might think they have to act tough, too."

"I guess." I shrugged. "I'm not sure."

"Why not try to get to know them better? Like, ask them what their favorite color is or something," Kara suggested.

I snorted and put on a real dorky voice. "Hi, my name is Devin. What's your favorite color? Do you want to come to my house after practice for a sing-along?"

Kara cracked up. I'd been making some really goofy faces as I'd said that. "Okay, maybe that wasn't a good idea," she said after she finally stopped laughing. "But what about something else? To break the ice?"

I thought about it. "I guess it couldn't hurt to try talking to some of them. You could be right. Maybe they are just feeling intimidated. But I'm not asking them their favorite color."

"Try asking if they like puppies or kittens better," Kara suggested as she giggled.

"No. I've got it!" I put on the goofy face and voice again. "What's your favorite kind of cookie?"

"Chocolate chip!" Kara answered through her giggles. "And my favorite color is blue. You knew that already. But you don't really know anything about your new team-mates."

"True." It was my turn to drum my fingers on my desk as I thought. An idea started to take shape in my mind. "I do know one thing we have in common: soccer!"

CHAPTER ELEVEN

The next day Jessi's mom, Mrs. Dukes, drove us to Pinewood Rec Center for practice. She had on a really cute turquoise tracksuit and a baseball cap. "Since you guys are getting your exercise, I might as well get mine," she said. There was a walking path in the park next to the center. She tucked her iPod into her pocket. "But before I do that, I want to talk to Coach Darby."

Jessi groaned and buried her head in her hands as her mom walked off toward the coach.

"I had a couple of bruises after the scrimmage on Monday," Jessi said. "My mom noticed them today. They don't really hurt, but they are kind of gruesome-looking. Anyway, she got all upset. She said I didn't get hurt like that on the Kicks."

I looked over at Mrs. Dukes, who was smiling as she talked to Coach Darby. Coach Darby smiled back and nodded before replying, and soon Mrs. Dukes was walking back toward us.

"Have a great practice!" she said, and smiled. "I'll be waiting by the car."

"Mom!" Jessi said, concerned. "What did you say?"

"I'll discuss it with you later," Mrs. Dukes said calmly. "Now get going."

She popped the iPod buds into her ears before she started moving at a brisk pace toward the trail.

Jessi and I exchanged glances as we got to the field, but before we could say anything, Coach Darby blew her whistle.

"Listen up!" she barked. "We're going to change our warm-up today. We're going to focus on a basic one that will help prevent injury. I've had some complaints from parents lately that we're playing too rough." And then she looked right at me and Jessi.

I could see the eyes of all the girls looking at us. But my parents hadn't said anything to Coach, or had they?

Coach Darby instructed us to pass the ball to one another using our hands, jogging and moving around the field the entire time. We would then add in some slow kicks to gently stretch our muscles. I was familiar with this routine; we had done a variation before with Coach Flores.

"Nice going," Jamie said as she jogged past me. "Now we're back to kindergarten drills. If you can't handle this team, you should just quit."

I could feel my face get hot. I didn't reply to Jamie; it wasn't worth it. Jessi looked at me sympathetically. "Sorry if you're getting flak for what my mom said."

I shook my head. "Who knows? Maybe my parents said something too."

"Hey, they have every right to," Jessi said, defending our parents. "If one day I have kids and they come home all black-and-blue, I'd want answers."

I smiled, imagining Jessi as a fierce, protective mom. I wouldn't mess with her kids!

Although Jessi cheered me up, I was sick and tired of being on a team that didn't feel like a team. I decided now was the perfect time to try my icebreaker, the one I'd thought of after I'd talked to Kara the night before. When the Kicks did this same warm-up, we would call out the name of the person we would be passing the ball to. I had a better idea. When I got the ball, I decided to give it a shot.

"Hey, guys?" I said loudly but with a little hesitation. After all, this was a tough group. Unsmiling faces turned toward me, and I felt butterflies doing a cha-cha in my stomach, but I kept going.

"What if we say the name of our favorite soccer player before we pass the ball to one another?" I suggested. I got blank stares, but luckily I had filled Jessi in on my plan in the car. As I kept moving, holding the ball, I nodded at Jessi.

"Mia Hamm!" I said as I tossed the ball to her.

Jessi caught it and searched the faces in the group before her eyes settled on Mirabelle. She threw her the ball, saying "Abby Wambach" as it flew through the air.

Mirabelle caught it as she jogged. I held my breath, wondering if she would help us out.

"Alex Morgan," Mirabelle said before tossing the ball to the girl on her right. Unfortunately, that girl was Jamie!

"I can tell you who my least favorite soccer player is," Jamie said, smirking as she caught the ball. "It's Devin."

A few of the girls snickered, but mostly everyone was silent.

"And you think you're so great, Jamie?" Jessi asked angrily.

Uh-oh. This had not turned out how I had hoped.

Jamie just laughed, which made Jessi even madder. But Coach Darby, who had been on the other end of the field, blew her whistle and called us over.

Jessi glared as Jamie ran past her. Jamie was eager, as always, to be the first one to reach the coach.

I jogged next to Jessi. "Don't," I said. "She is sooooo not worth it." I didn't want Jessi to get into trouble by getting into an argument with Jamie. But it made me feel good that my friend had my back.

Jessi let out a big exhale. "I know, but she makes me so mad sometimes that I can't even think straight!"

As we lined up in front of Coach Darby, I was feeling pretty disappointed. I really had hoped my idea would break some of the tension on the team. At least Mirabelle had tried to help.

After we did some extra stretching, Coach Darby had

us count off for a scrimmage. Jessi and I were on the same team this time (we had finally figured out not to stand next to each other!), and Jamie was on the opposite side.

We were once again nine on nine. "Sasha and Jessi, play forward," Coach said as she assigned positions. I was one of the four defenders. I tried not to overthink why Coach hadn't put me in as a striker. After all, it was only a practice scrimmage. But it did make me feel a little less confident.

Mirabelle and Jamie were both strikers on the opposing team. Mirabelle was good, consistently breaking free and dribbling her way through our defense. She scored the first goal.

Two defenders doubled up on Mirabelle, leaving me with Jamie. I stuck to her like glue.

"Move it!" Jamie hissed at me under her breath, frustrated that no one would pass her the ball because I was in the way. But I held my ground.

Tracey, playing midfield, shot a long, controlled pass to Jessi, who zipped past a defender and sent the ball sailing over the goalie's head.

"Nice pass! Nice goal!" I shouted out to them. Jessi grinned at me and gave me a thumbs-up.

I heard Jamie groan next to me. I'll admit it—that made me smile.

As Jamie raced around the field, trying to lose me, I kept up with her, enjoying every second of it. It was almost like part of me knew which way she was going to turn before she even moved. A couple of times I was there before she was! I didn't have much experience playing defense, but I was enjoying it. Although I'd always want to be a forward, it was nice to know I could do well in another position. Maybe trying to get the best of Jamie had something to do with how well I was playing.

After Mirabelle scored one more time, Jamie was practically foaming at the mouth to get a chance at the ball. She darted right, and I did too. If she took a step left, I was there.

"Devin, get away from me!" Jamie growled before suddenly whirling toward me, her arms outstretched. She shoved me with all her strength right in my chest, and I went down hard and landed flat on my back.

"Oof," I said as I looked up at the blue sky. The breath had been knocked from me and I couldn't move. I heard Coach's whistle blow and saw Jessi leaning over me, peering at me with concern.

"Devin, are you okay?" she asked.

I nodded as I tried filling my lungs with air. Yep, they still worked. "I'm okay. Just got the wind knocked out of me," I said as Jessi gave me a hand up.

As I stood, I saw Coach Darby talking to Jamie.

"Jamie, that was too much," Coach Darby said. "Dial it back a little, okay?"

Wow. It was good to know that some things were too much, even for Coach Darby. I heard Jamie muttering softly in reply. I couldn't make out what she was saying or what Coach Darby said in return before Coach came over to me, a concerned look on her face.

"Are you okay, Devin?" she asked.

"I'm fine," I said, putting on a face like I didn't care that Jamie had just been a total jerk. I tried to play it cool.

"Good." She nodded curtly. "Your dad told me you were having some issues with the rough play. But you were doing a great job out there, Devin. Sometimes things can get a little rough. Don't let it get to you."

So Dad had talked to Coach. That was a surprise. And I was in for another surprise too.

As I nodded and turned to go, Coach stopped me. "Jamie has something to say to you," she said.

Jamie walked over stiffly, not looking me in the eyes. "Sorry," she mumbled, looking at the ground.

Coach blew her whistle. "Time to cool down!" she yelled as she strode into the middle of the field.

As soon as Coach left, Jamie glared at me.

"What's it like being a tattletale, Devin?" she asked before stomping away.

Once again I didn't answer her. No matter what I said, it would never matter to Jamie!

CHAPTER TWELVE

"Why didn't you tell me you talked to Coach Darby?" I asked Dad as soon as we sat down to dinner that night.

Dad and Mom looked at each other.

"I meant to, Devin, but we've all been so busy," Dad said. "I guess it came up at practice?"

I nodded. "Jessi's mom talked to her too, and Coach brought it up in front of everybody. And Jamie called me a tattletale."

"Well, I'm sorry about that," Dad said. "But I'm curious. I talked to Coach Darby because I was concerned that you girls were playing too roughly and she wasn't stopping it. So how did she handle that today?"

I pushed my fork around on my plate, arranging the chicken-fried brown rice into a little mountain. "Well, she had us do some drills to prevent injury. And when Jamie pushed me during the scrimmage, Coach called her out."

Mom's eyes widened. "She pushed you?"

"She's the worst," I said.

Dad frowned. "Well, I'm glad to hear that Coach Darby took action. I wish that she had talked to you girls about unsportsmanlike conduct, though."

I shrugged.

"At least you had soccer practice," Maisie complained loudly, pieces of rice flying out of her mouth. "Some people don't get to play soccer at all. And some people have sisters who don't practice with them like they promised. And some people—"

"Maisie!" My dad cut her off. "May I remind you that some people should not speak with food in their mouth? Actually, that goes for all people. Especially the ones who live in this house."

Maisie put a hand over her mouth. "Oops. I forgot," she said from under it. Then she started chewing furiously, before swallowing superloudly. She took her hand away before launching into her tirade again.

"I don't get it. At least Devin has soccer. And she said she was going to help me, and she didn't do anything!" Maisie whined.

I felt a stab of guilt. I *had* promised to help my little sister, but I had been so busy with the winter league that I hadn't had a chance to figure out what to do yet. But Maisie didn't have to be such a brat about it. And I had bought her that cute puppy soccer key chain with my own money to try to cheer her up. Had she forgotten all about that? So instead of feeling guilty, I got angry.

"Maybe because it would be a big waste of my time," I

said in a really nasty voice. I couldn't help myself. I was feeling so angry and annoyed. "It's not like you're a real soccer player or anything. You haven't even played before."

Maisie's big eyes filled with tears. "Mom!" she cried.

I saw my parents look at each other and shake their heads before my dad turned to me. "Devin, you are clearly not interested in eating," he said, gesturing at my plate of uneaten food. "Please clear your plate and go up to your room. I'll be up in a few minutes."

I pushed back in my chair loudly, grabbed my plate, and stomped over to the kitchen with it. I was acting mad, but truthfully, I was feeling embarrassed over losing my temper with Maisie like that. I sprinted up the stairs and slammed the door to drown out the sound of Maisie complaining about me to my mom.

I jumped onto the bed and landed on my stomach, burrowing my face into my pillow. So what if Maisie couldn't play soccer? I was playing in the toughest league of my life, and it was a lot harder than I had anticipated. Not only did I have to deal with unfriendly teammates, but my own best friends seemed to be going in different directions. Frida wasn't even in school anymore! And while dealing with all of that, I was supposed to help my little sister too? I was feeling good and sorry for myself, so sorry that I had forgotten I had been the one who'd wanted to help Maisie. I could hear my family downstairs, my mom talking in a low voice to my sister as my dad cleared the table.

I heard footsteps coming up the stairs. I hoped it wasn't Maisie. I wasn't ready to apologize to her yet, and I knew that was what my parents would expect me to do. There was a light knock on the door before it opened. My dad stuck his head in.

"Want to kick the soccer ball around?" he asked.

I unstuck my head from my pillow. "Okay," I said, still a little sulky.

"Meet you in the backyard," my dad said cheerfully, as if I hadn't just yelled at Maisie and stormed off from the dinner table.

I got off the bed and laced up my sneakers, already feeling a little bit better. It was always fun to play soccer with my dad.

He was in the backyard, tapping the ball around when I got there. He had never played on a team, but he was a big soccer fan who sometimes played soccer on weekends with his friends. He passed the ball to me, and I tapped it back to him at an angle. He started running, and together we jogged the length of the backyard, tapping the ball back and forth to each other. I started to relax as I focused on this easy soccer drill.

"So," my dad said as we moved, "anything else you want to talk about?"

I had the ball, and I started to tap it back and forth as fast as I could between my feet, moving as quickly as possible until I started to tire myself out. I flipped the ball up and started tapping it up repeatedly on the instep of my right foot.

"Well," I said slowly as I watched the ball bounce. It was funny how sometimes I didn't feel like talking at all, and

Dad walked over and put his arm around me. "Those are three big problems, Devin. No wonder you are feeling stressed out. Remember, it always helps to talk about how you're feeling. Now, that's something you can learn from your sister," he said with a chuckle.

I laughed. "We all know exactly how Maisie is feeling every second of the day," I said.

"As far as the winter league goes, hang in there," Dad said. "Let me know if the roughness issue continues. And remember, it's only for a little while, and you'll be back playing with the Kicks again soon."

That was exactly what Steven had said! I needed to remember that.

"You know, it hasn't been all bad," I admitted to Dad, thinking about some of the things I had learned. "I am learning to play more aggressively, but I also ended up with my first yellow card ever!" I shuddered, still embarrassed by the thought.

"It's good to be assertive on the soccer field. That's the kind of aggression you want to channel, not the kind that gets you yellow cards," Dad said. "So stick with it, and I bet you'll keep learning and growing as a soccer player. At the end of the day, all you can do is keep playing your best," he continued. "You can't control the other girls on the team or the coach. Just keep being the best Devin you can be. Which, in my opinion, is always pretty awesome."

I smiled. "Thanks, Dad."

"As for your friends, make sure you keep communication

then all of a sudden the words would come pouring out, like a waterfall. That was what was about to happen.

"The winter league is really hard, the girls are really competitive, and you know I didn't even get to play at all that one game," I said as I let the ball roll off my foot. I planted my foot on top of it and put my hands on my hips as I continued. "There's no teamwork. Plus, Zoe isn't on our team and Emma and Frida aren't in the league at all. I feel like I might be losing some of my friends. So I was feeling pretty bummed about all that when Maisie started in about her soccer team." I thought about that. "Or, rather, about her *not* having a soccer team. She's right. I did say I would help her. There is just too much going on!"

My dad nodded sympathetically. "The straw that broke the camel's back, huh?"

"Exactly," I said.

"So if I've got this straight, you've got three things you're struggling with right now," Dad said. He began a recap. "One, the new league is very competitive and your teammates are not that friendly. Is that right?" he asked me. I thought of Jamie. "Not friendly" was putting it mildly, but sure, I'd go with that. I nodded. "Second, not all of your friends are on your team, and some of them aren't playing soccer at all right now. You're worried how this might affect your friendships." Again I nodded. "And, last, you wanted to help your sister find a way to play soccer because her program was canceled, but you haven't had the time. Does that sum it all up?"

"Yep," I said sadly.

open with them," he suggested. "Talk directly to them about how you're feeling, and be honest. It's the best way to avoid drama. Trust me. At my ripe old age, I know." He laughed.

"As for Maisie, I think it's nice that you want to help your little sister." Dad smiled warmly at me. "But don't put too much pressure on yourself. Do what you can, when you can. She'll be happy if you take her out to kick the soccer ball around every once in a while. Saving a school's entire soccer program is a tall order, Devin."

Then he looked at me and shook his head. "Although, you did save the Kangaroos and turn that team around. If anyone could save the elementary school soccer program, it would be you."

I felt better already. Suddenly my problems didn't seem that big and bad anymore.

"You know," Dad said thoughtfully as he kicked the ball out from under my foot before he started moving with it, "if you could conquer all three of these problems, it would be a real hat trick!"

A hat trick was when a player scored three goals in one game. A flawless hat trick was when a player scored three goals in a row in the same game.

I felt my confidence soaring, all thanks to my dad.

He kicked the ball toward me high, setting me up for a header. As I jumped into the air to meet it, I yelled out, "I'm gonna go for flawless!"

CHAPTER THIRTEEN

When I woke up the next day, I grabbed my phone right away to check for my morning text from Kara. When I'd lived in Connecticut, Kara and I had always picked out our outfits together. Since I'd moved, and with the three-hour time difference, we couldn't do that anymore, but instead, every morning Kara sent me a selfie of what she was wearing. After I got dressed, I did the same.

It might snow today! Kara had texted along with her photo. She wore a striped purple sweater hoodie, jeans, and a pair of silver fur-lined boots with cute little pom-poms hanging off the back. A headband with a sparkly snowflake on it pulled her long brown hair away from her face.

I felt a pang of jealousy. Although I loved the warm, sunny Southern California weather, I used to always look forward to the first snow of the year, even if it was just a dusting. When the whole world was covered in white, everything looked so pretty.

But then I thought of the cold. And wet shoes and gloves. And no soccer. So I cheered up as I slipped on my flip-flops. No way could Kara wear these in New England right now!

I posed in front of my floor-length mirror, making a funny face as I snapped a pic to send to Kara. I wore a pink baseball tee with the number thirteen on it. Mom had found it for me, and since thirteen was my jersey number on the Kicks, she'd known I would love it. My long brown hair was usually stick-straight, but today it hung in beachy waves around my shoulders. After I'd taken a shower the night before, I'd put my wet hair in braids. When I'd taken the braids out this morning, my hair had had a nice wave. Not as fabulous as Frida's curls, but I liked it.

After I texted Kara, I sent a text to Jessi, Zoe, and Emma, asking them all to meet me in the courtyard at lunch. Talking with my dad last night had put me in a really good mood. A hat trick! I could do it. And I was going to start with an easy goal, one that I knew my friends would assist me on.

So I was all smiles as I waited in the courtyard behind the library building, at the table we always sat at whenever we ate outside. Zoe was the first one to sit down. She gave her usual shy smile as she looked at me from under her side-swept bangs.

"Hey, Devin," she said as she slid her cafeteria tray onto

the table in front of her. She had a slice of pizza, a bottle of water, and an apple.

"Hi, Zoe!" I said cheerfully as I dug out my own lunch bag. I wondered what Mom had in store for me today. I breathed a sigh of relief when I saw turkey on pita bread with hummus. That was one of my favorite sandwiches, and I took it as a good omen that things were going to go my way.

Emma and Jessi walked into the courtyard together and sat down next to us. The sun was shining, and it was nice and warm, a perfect day to eat outside.

"Kara told me it might snow in Connecticut today," I told them. They had all met Kara when she'd come for a visit to watch the Kicks play in a rematch against Pinewood a couple of months before.

Zoe's eyes lit up. "The hats! The scarves and boots! I love winter accessories, and I never get to wear them."

Emma shivered. "Not me. I'm happy I live in a place where it's warm. I get mad at my brothers when they turn the air-conditioning too high."

"I think it would be fun to be in a snowstorm. I'd love to have a snowball fight," Jessi added.

"It is fun, until you get plowed in the face with a snowball," I told them. Everyone laughed, and I figured it was the perfect way to start the conversation, on a high note. "So thanks for coming! I know we haven't all eaten lunch together in a while."

Zoe and Emma both looked around nervously, like I

was going to try to make them feel bad or something,

"Hey! It's okay." I held my hands up in the air, the *I come in peace* move I used a lot with Maisie. "Things changed when we tried out for the winter league. But we'll always be friends. And friends should be able to talk about things, so I thought maybe we could do that today."

Emma leaned back in her chair. "You know what? That's a great idea, Devin. Do you mind if I say something first?"

"Please do," I said, relieved that Emma at least seemed willing to talk right away.

"Thanks," she said before she took a deep breath. She looked a little nervous. "I know you all were trying to be nice to me about not making the soccer league. And my 'Emma Is Excellent' day was so fun. I'm sorry I got mad when Steven and Cody showed up and you guys started talking about soccer. I just felt so left out."

"We get it," Jessi said as she smiled encouragingly at Emma. "I couldn't even imagine if I didn't make the team and you guys did. I don't know if I'd be able to even watch soccer again."

I shuddered, putting myself in Emma's place. "That would totally stink."

"So that's why I've been hanging with the Tree Huggers," Emma explained. "It just felt good to not have to be reminded of not making the team, you know?"

We all nodded. "It's okay, but the Tree Huggers have to be your second-best friends, not your very best friends, okay?" Zoe said.

"Awwww, of course!" Emma launched herself across the table to hug Zoe, knocking over Zoe's water bottle, which had the top off. We all screamed and scrambled to move our backpacks and notebooks out of the way of the rushing water. Emma began sheepishly mopping it up with some napkins.

"At least it's just water, right?" she asked in her typical cheerful manner as we all cracked up.

After the water had been cleaned up, Emma stood up and insisted on an official group hug. "Let's do one where I can't do any damage!" she said, holding out her arms.

"Um, maybe we should see if the school has a padded room somewhere?" Jessi joked.

We all laughed as we had a big hug fest. When Emma untangled herself from our arms, she had a serious look on her face. "I want to make one thing clear. I don't expect you guys not to talk about soccer at all around me. I want to be a good friend, the kind you can tell anything to. I want to support you. But I'm just asking you not to talk all soccer, all the time, okay?"

"Of course!" I said, and soon we were all hugging again.

After we sat back down, Zoe had something to say. "I hope you don't mind if I eat lunch with the other Gators every now and then. We like to talk strategy and go over games."

"And we do have Tree Hugger meetings sometimes during lunch," Emma reminded us.

"Hey, we all should be able to have different interests

and still be friends," Jessi said. "We'd be totally boring if we all did and liked the exact same things all the time."

"We should do something that's just the four of us," I suggested. "Or just the five of us, when Frida gets back."

"It is so weird not having her around. I miss her," Zoe said. "Especially in my English class. She used to put on all these funny accents whenever she had to read something out loud."

At that moment all of our phones beeped at the same time. We looked—it was another group text from Frida.

"That girl is psychic!" Jessi remarked.

We opened the text to see a photo of a chili dog loaded with melted cheese and onions.

Can you believe what Brady eats for lunch? Frida asked.

"Oh my gosh, he must have terrible breath!" Zoe said.

"Never!" Emma said. "Brady's breath is like . . . peppermints and rainbows and a fresh summer breeze."

Jessi, Zoe, and I shook our heads.

"How would you know what Brady's breath is like, anyway?" Jessi asked.

Emma sighed. "Someday I will. I know it."

Frida's text had given me an idea.

"Hey!" I said loudly. "Remember when we were talking about helping to raise money for Maisie's school, so they could get the soccer program going? Maybe that's something we could all do together—even Frida."

Emma smiled. "That sounds like fun! I'm in!"

"Me too!" Jessi chimed in.

"And me!" Zoe added. "Even though Frida's not around, we could ask her for ideas. We can text and video chat with her, so it will be like she's a part of it too."

"That's exactly what I was thinking," I said.

"So let's all brainstorm some ideas, and maybe we can get together this weekend to share them," Jessi said. "How does that sound?"

"Perfect!" I said out loud. But inside I was thinking, *Goal!* One down, two to go.

CHAPTER FOURTEEN

I felt cheerful and relaxed before practice that day—a first for the winter league! Knowing that Emma, Zoe, Jessi, and I were all in this together, even if we weren't all playing together, made me feel better than I had in a while. Which gave me the confidence to try yet another icebreaker at practice that afternoon.

After we had warmed up, again focusing on stretches to prevent injury, we ran a few drills before we divided up for a scrimmage. This time Coach Darby split us into teams.

"Amanda, I want you to start on goal," she said. "Lauren, Sasha, and Kelly, you're on defense. Midfield is Meg, Kristin, and Sarah. I want Devin and Jessi on the forward line. Got it?"

We nodded as Coach strode over to the other team to assign positions. I jumped up and down with excitement.

I had been worried that since Coach Darby had praised me on defense, she would keep me there. But I was back as a striker!

"I am so happy Jamie isn't on our team," Jessi said as she glanced across the field, sticking out her tongue.

"Me too," I said. "Which makes what I'm about to do a lot easier."

Jessi looked at me quizzically as I cupped my hands around my mouth. "Hey, anyone want to do something fun to warm up?"

"Sure!" Jessi answered cheerfully right away, but everyone else looked around hesitantly, until Sarah, one of the Kicks, stepped up.

"Why not?" she said.

Everyone else shrugged. I heard an unenthusiastic "Okay" and a "Sure."

It wasn't a glowing response, but it was better than nothing. I seized the opportunity and barreled forward.

"I'll start," I said. "First, I'll do a cartwheel." I jumped and sprang off my hands to demonstrate.

"Then I'll pick another person to do a cartwheel." I looked around like I was deciding, but I already knew who it would be. "Jessi!" Jessi did a perfect cartwheel.

"Then Jessi picks someone," I said, and Jessi called out, "Sarah!"

Sarah turned the cartwheel, but a little shakily. "I'm not the best at cartwheels," she said, and laughed. Everyone started chatting as Sarah said, "Amanda."

As Amanda did her cartwheel, I explained the rest of the warm-up. "If you get called more than once, you have to do an extra cartwheel. So if Jessi gets called again, she'll have to do two cartwheels in a row. If she gets called a third time, then she'll have to do three."

Everyone watched their teammates attempting cartwheels. Some were a lot better than others. Kelly took a running start and then sprang off her hands, but her legs barely left the ground. "Did I do it?" she asked. "It felt like I did!"

Jessi shook her head. "Sorry to break it to you, but no," she said as everyone, including Kelly, laughed. It was nice to see one of the most competitive players on the team loosen up and have a little fun.

We were having such a good time that I barely noticed the other team, but I looked over at one point and saw Jamie smirking at us. She elbowed Stephanie and jerked her chin in our direction, but Stephanie looked over and away again without responding to Jamie. I saw Jamie's cheeks get red, and I couldn't be sure but she looked a little embarrassed to me. It made me feel good that Stephanie didn't join in on Jamie's mocking of us. And if Jamie felt self-conscious in the process, oh well!

Coach Darby's whistle blew, and we were on the field. We received the ball first, Courtney kicking it deep into our midfield. Sarah stopped it with her foot and began moving it down the left side, but Jamie and Stephanie charged for her. Stephanie stole it out from under Sarah

and passed it to Jamie down the field. She started dribbling it toward the goal, and I figured she'd have a good
shot. But then Kelly zoomed in front of her and kicked
it away. It went out of bounds, and Jamie shot Kelly an
irritated look.

"Go, Kelly!" I heard Lauren shout. That was a first. The
Griffons usually played without a lot of talking. As the
scrimmage went on, I noticed our communication was a
lot better on the field, the best it had ever been. It seemed
to be helping a lot.

At one point I had the ball but was surrounded by
defense.

"Devin! Over here! Over here!" Kristin was running
parallel to me, and there was a slight opening. I passed the
ball to her, and she moved it down, finding an opening to
pass it to Jessi, who kicked the ball right into the goal and
over Courtney's head.

At one point Jessi got the ball from Mirabelle and
kicked it to me. I charged down the field and zeroed in
on the goal. I was going to do this, and nothing could stop
me! Until I felt a shove that sent my feet flying as I lost
control of the ball. It was Jamie, who took the ball from
me and moved it away from the goal.

I heard Coach Darby's whistle blow. "Offsides!" she
shouted. "And a yellow card for Jamie!"

Wow, finally, I thought. It looked like hearing from
some of the parents had gotten to Coach Darby.

The next time Jamie had the ball, she found herself

surrounded by our defense. She tried to elbow her way through, but Kelly and Lauren weren't budging, so she was forced to kick the ball wildly across the field, hoping one of her teammates could get it.

I was all over it! I intercepted it and took off running straight down the middle of the field, so fast that the other team couldn't catch me. When I was in striking distance of the goal, I kicked the ball hard and fast, trying for not too high and not too low. Courtney jumped up to catch it, but it only brushed her fingertips as it went into the goal.

Kristin, who was the closest player to me, ran over for a high five. "Way to go, Devin!" she said, and she actually smiled. Wow!

The play continued, with Mirabelle making a goal for the other team and Jessi making one more for our team. At the end, we were the winners, 3–1. There was a lot of high-fiving and smiling on our team. The vibe had shifted, even if it was just a little bit, and I was feeling pretty good—until Coach Darby walked over to me.

"Devin," she said in her no-nonsense voice. "What did you have the girls doing before the game?"

Uh-oh. Was she going to be mad? Was this going to be like the socks all over again?

"W-well," I stammered, full of nerves. "It was just an icebreaker to get us communicating."

"Hmmmm," Coach Darby said, deep in thought. "It looks like it helped with that, but it also really unnerved the other team when they were watching you. It gave you the competitive edge. I like that. Maybe we can try something like that at the next game." She patted me on the shoulder. "Good job."

I smiled, and then Kelly walked by.

"Great game, Devin," she said.

That was the first time Kelly had said anything nice to me—or for that matter, anything at all. It looked like my icebreaker was helping with our teamwork issue after all.

I didn't feel quite like I had made the second goal in my hat trick yet. But the goal was in my sights, and I now knew some of my teammates were ready to assist!

CHAPTER FIFTEEN

"Thanks for helping me out with this," I said to Jessi, Emma, and Zoe on Friday afternoon. They had come to my house to help me teach Maisie how to play soccer.

"No problem," said Zoe. "I'm just glad we could find a time when we could all be together."

"It almost didn't work out," I told her. "Demolition Darby nearly stuck us with an extra practice today."

Jessi cracked up. "Demolition Darby? That's too good."

I grinned. "Yeah, it's perfect."

"Is that what you call her?" Emma asked. "I'm starting to think it's a good thing I didn't make this league!"

Just then Mom pulled up in the driveway with Maisie and two of her friends, Kaylin and Juliet. Kaylin wore her dark hair in braids, and Juliet had short blond hair.

"Oh my gosh, it's Maisie and a little Jessi and a little Zoe!" Emma said, and I realized that they did kind of look like younger versions of our friends. "Is there a little Emma in there too?"

Mom laughed. "No, just these three mini-Kicks."

"Kaylin and Juliet want to play soccer too, so Mom said they could come," Maisie said, as if she were expecting me to complain about it.

"That's great!" I said. "The more players we have, the better the drills will be. Come on. We're all set up in the backyard."

"All set up" sounded much more impressive than it was. My friends had brought their soccer balls, and Dad had gotten us some cones when I'd told him we would need them for practice. But it would be enough to help Maisie learn soccer.

Jessi and I had been talking about the drills we remembered doing when we were kids, so we'd come up with a plan.

"Okay, let's everybody get in a circle!" I said. "We're going to play a game."

Maisie put her hands on her hips. "I'm not here to play games. I'm here to learn soccer!"

I looked at Jessi and rolled my eyes, but it was Emma who straightened her out.

"Lighten up, mini-Devin!" she said. "Playing games is a great way to learn stuff."

"Okay," Maisie said. "But don't call me mini-Devin!"

"Yes, please don't!" I added.

We all formed a circle, and I launched into the game.

"Okay, this game is called I Can Do—Can You?" I began. "I'm going to do something, and then you guys have to copy me. Okay?"

Maisie and her friends nodded. I started by doing jumping jacks.

"I can do jumping jacks. Can you?" I asked.

"Of course!" Maisie yelled, and her friends giggled as they did their jumping jacks.

Then I nodded to Jessi, who took over. "I can hop on one foot. Can you?" And we all started hopping on one foot.

I hadn't realized it when I was doing this as a kid, but when my coach back then had played this game with us, she'd been teaching us balance and movement. After Jessi, Emma, Zoe, and I all gave challenges, we let the girls challenge us.

"I can stand on my hands, can you?" asked Maisie, doing a perfect handstand.

"Um, I'm too tall to do a handstand," Emma said, giving it her best try.

"If you can't do it, we win!" Maisie said.

"Maisie, this isn't about winning. It's about having fun," I said, rolling my eyes at Jessi again. I was starting to wonder if helping Maisie was such a good idea.

"Let's play Hit the Cone!" Jessi shouted, and she made it sound like so much fun that the three little girls cheered.

We scattered the cones around the backyard and gave each girl a ball.

"When I say go, I want you to dribble the ball to a cone and then try to hit the cone with the ball," said Jessi.

"That's easy," said Maisie.

"Go!" Jessi yelled.

The girls started dribbling the balls around the yard. They were so cute, all of them concentrating really hard. The balls kept getting away from them, like it had for me when I'd first been learning how to dribble.

"Short kicks!" I coached them. "And wait until you get close to the cone before you hit it."

"Got one!" yelled Juliet (aka mini-Zoe), and I saw Maisie frown. I knew she had wanted to be the first to hit the cone.

Jessi caught the look too. "I hope she turns out to be a mini-Devin and not a mini-Jamie," she said to me.

"I hope so too!" I said. "We're going to have to do some good sportsmanship games with them or something."

I was about to jump in and give the girls some dribbling tips when a voice rang across the backyard.

"Did you miss me?"

I whirled around and saw Frida giving Emma a huge hug! I had texted Frida about today but hadn't heard back.

"Surprise!" Frida said when she saw me. "They let us off set early today, so I came right over."

Frida's red curls were the shiniest I had ever seen them, and her face looked polished and perfect.

"Are you wearing your set makeup?" Zoe asked. "You look like a high schooler!"

"It's for the cameras," Frida said. "You'll see. When the movie comes out, I'll look just like regular old me on the screen."

Maisie abandoned her ball and ran up to greet Frida.

"Frida! What are you today? A wizard? A detective? A princess?" she asked.

Maisie was Frida's biggest fan when Frida played for the Kicks. Maisie always wanted to know what character Frida was playing when she was on the field.

"Well, right now I'm playing middle school girl who just spent an exciting day filming a TV movie with an adorable superstar, Brady McCoy," Frida answered.

Kaylin and Juliet came running over.

"Do you know Brady McCoy?" Kaylin asked, wide-eyed.

"Kaylin likes him!" Juliet said with a giggle.

"Well, we're currently working together," Frida said, as if she were being interviewed by *Hollywood Tonight* and not by a bunch of eight-year-olds in a backyard.

"What's he like?" Emma asked. "You so owe me details!"

"Well, he's always on time, and he knows his lines, and between takes he likes to practice his dance moves," Frida reported.

"And can you confirm that his favorite color is teal? And that his favorite food is spaghetti Bolognese? And his favorite dog is a yellow Lab? Because that's what all the magazines say, but sometimes I wonder if they make that stuff up," Emma said.

"Well, none of that stuff has ever come up in

conversation," Frida said. "But he showed me a picture of his dog on his phone, and I think it was yellow."

"He showed you his phone?" Emma squealed, and then Kaylin, Maisie, and Juliet started squealing too.

"Enough about Brady," Frida said. "I came to help teach Maisie how to play soccer."

"Can you tell us how to act when we're on the soccer field, like you do?" Maisie asked.

"Well, sure," Frida said. She looked at the cones. "What were you guys doing when I came up? It looks like fun."

"We just have to hit the cones with the ball, but it's not as easy as it sounds," Maisie said.

"They need a little help with ball control," Jessi said.

Frida nodded. "I think I got it. You guys are spies, all right? And if you hit the ball with the cone, you will gain entrance into this bad guy's secret lab. But if you lose the ball, his goons will detect you, so you have to be really focused. Got it?"

Maisie nodded. "Spies. Got it."

"Why are we being spies?" Juliet asked.

"Just try it," Maisie said.

The three girls started dribbling the ball again with super-serious looks on their faces. They moved a little more slowly and carefully this time.

Now it was my turn to hug Frida. "I'm so glad you came!" I said.

"Me too," said Frida. "I miss you guys like crazy. But filming will be done soon."

"So, you're saying that time is running out for me to meet Brady in person?" Emma asked, and Zoe nudged her.

Frida rolled her eyes, but she was laughing. "Anyway, I'm glad I could make it," Frida said. "Maisie and her friends are supercute."

"Yeah, they are," I admitted.

"We've *got* to find a way to save their soccer program," Jessi said.

"I know," agreed Zoe. "Things have just been so crazy."

"Well, maybe we could meet after our games tomorrow and come up with a plan," I suggested. "We had some decent ideas the last time we talked."

"I think I can do it," said Zoe.

"Me too," added Emma.

Frida frowned. "We're shooting tomorrow. But I'll be there in spirit."

I hugged Frida. "And anyway, you're here now, right? The Kicks are back together again."

"What do you mean, back together?" Frida asked. "We're always together, even when we're not," she said, and I totally got it.

Soccer or no soccer, we would always be the Kicks. We would always be there for one another. Why hadn't I figured that out sooner?

I should have realized my friends would help me make this hat trick easy!

CHAPTER SIXTEEN

"Are we there yet?" Maisie whined in the seat next to me.

It was Saturday morning, early, and the Griffons were playing the Gilmore Giants all the way out in Los Arboles. This time the whole family was coming to the game, which meant I got stuck in the backseat with Maisie instead of being able to sit up front next to Dad. I had my headphones on for a while, but I was ramped up about the game, and the music was distracting. But it was less distracting than Maisie.

"We're almost there," Mom said, and then I slipped my headphones back on and looked out the window.

Were we driving all this way just so I could sit on a bench again? And if I did get to play, would I turn into some kind of aggro beast and start elbowing players on the field? I imagined a sea of yellow cards raining down from the sky.

Or what if I kept my cool but I got hit—or worse, hurt? What if I got an injury that kept me out of soccer for the season? Or for the Kicks' season? Or for the rest of my life?

I knew my thoughts were out of control, so I took a deep breath and looked out the window again. The last practice had gone pretty well. Coach Darby had let me play striker. And the Griffons were starting to come together as a team—well, most of the Griffons, anyway.

It had to be a better game, right?

I had my first clue that things were on the upswing when I got onto the field. Jessi jogged up to me, and I saw her mom and dad waving to us from the sidelines.

"Hey, Devin," Jessi said, stretching. She glanced over at the Giants, who were starting to warm up on the other side of the field in their navy-and-white uniforms. "From their name, I thought maybe they'd all be way taller than us. But they look like normal humans."

"Let's hope they play like normal humans," I said, and then Coach Darby walked onto the field.

"Listen up, girls!" she yelled. "Today Devin's going to lead us in a team building exercise. Get to it, Devin!"

I gave Jessi a wide-eyed look and jogged out in front of the other players.

"All right, some of you remember this from the other day," I said, feeling my confidence rise a little bit with each word. "I'll do a cartwheel and call out someone's name. If I call you, you do a cartwheel and call out another player's name. If your name gets called a second time, you have to do two cartwheels; if it gets called a third time, you do three, and so on. Got it?"

I saw Jamie roll her eyes, but most of the girls nodded. I did a cartwheel and decided that for the sake of teamwork, I should call on somebody I wasn't friends with on the team.

"Sasha!" I yelled, and Sasha launched right into her cartwheel without complaint.

"Jamie!" Sasha cried.

I almost expected Jamie to refuse, but this exercise had been the coach's idea, so Jamie performed the bounciest, springiest cartwheel I had ever seen.

The drill went perfectly, and I stopped after I was sure every player had been called out. Coach Darby seemed pleased.

"All right. Let's see some drills!" she yelled when we were done, and we began our usual warm-ups.

I didn't know if our cartwheels had intimidated the other team the way Coach Darby had hoped, but they'd definitely lightened the mood on our team. I mean, we were all serious, as usual, but everybody looked a little more relaxed, and I even saw some smiles.

Then it was time for Coach Darby to give us the starting lineup.

"Lauren, Beth Anne, Tracey, Sarah, defense!" she said. "Kelly, left wing. Jessi, right wing. Mirabelle and Devin, midfield center."

Devin! She'd called my name! I was so excited, I didn't

hear her call out the last three positions, but I wasn't surprised to see Courtney on goal and Jamie and Sasha as strikers.

I jogged onto the field, more determined than ever to stay focused, get the ball, and score. The whistle blew, and the next thing I knew, one of the Giants was stampeding toward the Griffons' goal.

Mirabelle and I raced up to meet her. Another Giant came out of nowhere and almost knocked me over just with her sheer momentum, but I saw her out of the corner of my eye and sidestepped her. As I did, Mirabelle got the ball away from the Giant and passed it to Jamie.

We followed Jamie down the field as she charged toward the goal. She had a clear shot, and she took it, but she was far outside the penalty box, and the ball slowed down as it got closer. The Giants' goalie jumped on it.

I knew Jamie had been showing off with that shot, but it didn't give me any pleasure that she'd missed it—she was on my team, and we needed the goal. But I did file away one useful bit of information: The Giants' defense on the left side of the field had been nowhere in sight when Jamie had taken her shot. So they had a weakness.

I kept that in mind the next time the ball came into my territory. I started dribbling it and veered left. Mirabelle had someone on her like glue, and Jamie was calling out for me to pass, but she had a defender right in front of her.

I moved even sharper left and found the pocket that

Jamie had taken before. I needed to get closer to the goal if I was going to score, but I could see two Giants heading toward me from the other side of the field. So I had to move fast.

I took the ball another ten yards and then, bam! I kicked it hard and low. The goalie dove for it, but she couldn't match its speed.

"Griffons score!" the ref yelled, and I got that feeling that you get only when you score, that feeling that your blood is pumping hard in your veins and you're as light as air and you can do anything. Sasha high-fived me as we got back into position.

The Giants came back hard, though, and their coach must have finally noticed that defensive hole, because they quickly sewed it up tight. Jamie and Sasha couldn't get near the goal, and the Giants scored twice before the half was over.

Coach Darby's face was like stone at halftime.

"They've tightened up their defense," she said. "You have to find a way to get through them. Look for openings. Be aggressive! Keep passing to confuse them. Don't try to be a hero and do it on your own. It will take a team to take the Giants down!"

We all let out a rousing cheer, pumped up for the game to continue.

"Devin, Stephanie, I want you on forward!" she said, and I was so happy, I bet my beaming could be seen from the stands. She kept Mirabelle and Jessi on the bench, though, and I noticed that Jamie wasn't starting the half—for the first time ever.

Back on the field I tried to keep Coach's strategy in mind. Confusing the defense sounded like a good idea. Sasha, Kelly, Zarine, and Meg were in midfield, and I tried to keep a mental note of their positions as the ball zigzagged between the teams.

Early in the second half, I intercepted the ball when two Giants tried to pass it to each other. I took it a few feet and saw Stephanie open sideways. I hit her with a short pass, and then Kelly jogged up next to her on the left. Stephanie passed it to Kelly.

Zarine had already raced ahead, so Kelly passed it to her. Stephanie and I made it to the goal. Two Giants defenders charged me, leaving Stephanie free. Zarine passed it to Stephanie—who lobbed it right past the goalie's head into the net! The score was tied!

"Great teamwork!" Coach Darby called out.

It looked as though Coach Darby had learned an important lesson about teamwork, and as the game continued, I was about to learn one myself about aggressive playing.

A loose ball was up for grabs close to me. I thought of what Coach Darby had said: "Be aggressive!" And I remembered what my dad had said about using the winter league as an opportunity to learn how to play more aggressively. Although the Giants were closing in on the ball, I swooped in, not afraid of contact but being careful at the same time not to foul. I felt fearless, and I didn't know if it was my imagination, but it felt like I was running faster on the field than I ever had before. I had a perfect shot at the goal, and I went for it, keeping the ball low to the ground and aiming it toward the right back post of the goal.

The Giants' goalie dove for it, but it was impossible for her to get all the way down to the ground and over to the post at the same time. I scored!

"Way to hustle, Devin!" Coach Darby shouted. I felt my teammates' hands clapping me on the back in congratulations. We kept up our strategy, but we couldn't manage to score again in the third quarter. Though, we didn't let the Giants score either. In the last quarter Coach Darby subbed Stephanie and me out and put Mirabelle and Jessi in our places.

I didn't mind being benched. I had already played well and scored two goals. Mirabelle and Jessi were rested. I couldn't wait to see what they would do on the field!

It didn't hurt that the two of them had been playing together since they were little kids. The way they passed the ball back and forth to each other as they glided down the field looked like some kind of choreographed dance. They were totally in tune with each other.

Finally Mirabelle set Jessi up with a perfect shot. Jessi aimed it right for the corner of the goal, and the goalie just didn't get to it in time.

"Griffons score!" the ref yelled.

Jessi's point ended up being the one we needed to win the game. We beat the Giants, 4–2. After we shook hands with the other team, I celebrated with a cartwheel.

When I was upright again, I saw an amazing sight. All of the Griffons were doing cartwheels! (Well, not Jamie.) Then everybody was laughing and hugging, and it was pretty awesome.

"This is what I expect from you guys!" Coach Darby barked, but I knew she was really pleased.

Then she dismissed us, and Jessi and I found our families on the sidelines.

"Can we take you girls out for a celebratory brunch?" Dad asked.

"That sounds nice, but we've got to meet Emma and Frida back home soon," I said. "I just completed the second part of my hat trick, but I've got one more to go."

Dad grinned. "Got it, Devin. Let's head back, and I'll pick up some pizzas for everyone on the way."

"Thanks!" I said, and nodded to Jessi. "See you at the house!"

Fixing my friendships and getting the Griffons to work as a team hadn't been as hard as I'd thought. But saving a soccer program—that was going to be the toughest trick yet!

CHAPTER SEVENTEEN

"Hey! There's tomato sauce on my binder!" Zoe said.

My friends and I were at the table in my backyard, eating pizza and starting to talk about our fund-raising plans. Zoe, as usual, had all her ideas neatly organized in a binder, along with pictures to show us.

"Sorry," Emma said. "I don't know what it is, but when I eat, it's like I get the food everywhere but in my mouth."

"Gross!" Zoe shrieked, and then we all started giggling. Then Zoe took a napkin and carefully cleaned off her binder.

"You know that cute key chain you got at the mall, Devin?" Zoe said. "Something like that shouldn't be too hard to make. I've been thinking about the craft fair idea. We could make a whole bunch of soccer-related crafts, or even sports-related crafts, and sell them. See, I found all these ideas online."

Zoe opened the binder and showed us some stuff she had printed out. There were cute little soccer ball necklaces with soccer balls made out of sculpting clay, and a little stuffed teddy bear made out of felt holding a soccer ball.

"Soooooo cute!" said Emma.

"Yeah, cool," said Jessi.

Zoe grinned. "Good, because I already made a bunch, and my sisters are helping too, and so are Mira and Tamika from my team."

I was impressed. "Wow, Zoe, that's awesome."

"Well, my dad said he'd bake his famous coconut cakes for us to sell," Jessi said. "I was thinking we could do a bake sale."

"Oh my gosh, yum!" Emma said. "Your dad's coconut cake is the best."

I jumped in. "That's great. My idea was to do a soccer clinic for kids. Kind of like the one we did with Maisie and her friends, but with more kids, and we could charge a small fee."

"That is genius," Zoe said, and I smiled. I thought so too.

"Well, I was talking to the Tree Huggers about it, and they want to help us," Emma said. "We've been research-ing a way to wash cars without a lot of water, and without polluting the water supply. We thought maybe we could wash cars to raise money for the soccer program. It would be educational, too."

"Aw, that's sweet! Then you'll have to change your name to the Soccer Huggers," Zoe joked.

Emma squeezed her. "I'm a Soccer Hugger, and I'm proud of it!"

"These are all amazing ideas," I said. "It's going to be hard to pick one."

"Why do we have to pick just one?" Jessi asked. "Can't we do all of them?"

Zoe nodded. "Or better yet, do them all in the same place at the same time. I already checked with the Kentville Community Center about doing a craft sale, and they said next Saturday is open."

"We could call it a Save the Soccer League Fair!" I said, excited. Then it hit me. "Wait, next Saturday? Don't we have a game?"

Jessi shook her head. "Next week's game is on Sunday. So it would work out. But it's not a lot of time to prepare."

"I know," Zoe agreed. "But it wouldn't be too hard. We've got this afternoon free, right? After we confirm with the community center, we can make posters and start putting them up around town."

"And online, too," Emma said.

Jessi picked up her phone. "I'd better tell my dad to start baking!"

"We'll need more volunteers to bake," Devin said. "And if you guys are busy with your stuff, I'll need help running the soccer clinic."

"I'll help you," Jessi said. "I'll get my dad to run the bake sale table."

"Why don't we ask the other Kicks?" Zoe said. "I'll ask Grace. Zarine and Sarah are on the Griffons with you, right? I bet they'd help."

I nodded. "Yeah. Hey, we could ask the other Griffons too."

Jessi raised an eyebrow. "*All* the Griffons?"

"Well, maybe not Jamie," I said, reading her mind. "But I bet some of them will help. It's worth a try. I mean, they're our teammates, and teammates help one another, right?"

Jessi shook her head. "Devin, you were born to be a team captain, you know that?"

I think I blushed a little at Jessi's compliment. I liked hearing it. That was one of my dreams—that I would be playing on a big field one day, maybe even in the World Cup, leading my team to victory. Hey, I could dream, right?

"So, I think we have a plan," Zoe said. "I have the number for the community center lady. I'll call her."

"Devin, can we use your laptop?" Emma asked. "I have an amazing idea for the poster."

"Sure," I said, and I went inside, feeling really good. We were within goal range of saving Maisie's soccer program. For the first time I felt like we could really do it!

"So, basically we would do some fun drills with the kids, and the money would go toward the elementary school soccer program," I told some of my teammates on Monday at practice as we warmed up.

"That's an awesome idea," said Zarine. "Sarah and I can help. Right, Sarah?"

Sarah nodded. "Definitely."

"I'll help," Mirabelle said.

I smiled at her. "Thanks!"

Some of the other girls heard us talking, and I started explaining the whole plan over again. Katie, Tracey, and Kristin all said they could help too.

"What time do we have to be there?" Kristin asked.

"Well, we have the community center from eleven to four on Saturday, so anytime you can come would be great," I told them.

"What's this about making plans for Saturday?"

It was Coach Darby.

"Oh, hi, Coach," I said. "We're organizing a Save the Soccer League Fair to raise money for the elementary school league. There's no program right now because there's no funding."

Coach Darby frowned. "I was going to call for an extra practice on Saturday, so we'd be in shape for Sunday," she said, and my heart sank. But then she said something amazing. "Tell you what. We can have an early-morning Sunday practice. I think your fair is a good idea."

I beamed at her. "Thanks! It's at the Kentville Community Center. You should come."

"Maybe I will," she said. "Just don't forget about practice Sunday. Bright and early."

"No problem, Coach!" I said, and I could tell that I was smiling from ear to ear.

"Wow," Jessi said as Coach walked away.

"I know," I said. "So cool. I will always and forever be one of the Kicks at heart. But right now it feels pretty good to be a Griffon, too!"

CHAPTER EIGHTEEN

"Wow, this place looks amazing!" Emma said.

It was ten forty-five on the morning of the Save the Soccer League Fair. The whole week had been totally crazy! And we had all gotten to the center at seven in the morning to set up for the fair. I was tired already, but it was so worth it. Emma was right. The place looked amazing.

Outside, a big SAVE THE SOCCER LEAGUE FAIR banner hung over the doorway. Mom had made it and enlisted Maisie and her friends to help paint it. It looked super-sweet. On the center's side lawn we had tons of soccer balls and cones ready for the soccer clinic. Zarine, Sarah, and Grace were already there to help, kicking soccer balls around as they waited for things to begin. Since they were Kicks, I had known they would come out and support us, but I felt great when I saw that Griffons Katie, Tracey, and

Kristin were kicking the balls around with them too!

Over on the other side of the center, Emma's Tree Huggers were getting ready for their environmentally friendly car wash. The center had given them permission to hold the car wash on the grassy area next to the parking lot, so the dirty water wouldn't end up in the storm drain system. Michelle, one of the Tree Huggers, waved over Emma and me, a huge smile on her face. She held a bucket filled with a soapy liquid.

"It's a biodegradable, nontoxic cleaner," she said. "It uses very little water, and it doesn't streak, so we don't have to worry about rinsing. But we'll need to make up for it with a lot of elbow grease." She gestured to a pile of large sponges, one side soft and the other with scrubber surfaces on them. "We do the work, not the water!"

I was impressed that everyone, even people I didn't know that well, were willing to work so hard to help save the soccer program!

Inside, there were tables set up for the craft sale and the bake sale. Zoe's sisters and Jessi's dad had arrived and were making things look beautiful.

"It's perfect," I said. "There's only one thing left to do."

"What's that?" Jessi asked.

I grinned. "Sock swap!"

"I knew you were going to say that!" Emma cried, lifting up the leg of her jeans to show off a pair of bright purple-and-pink-striped socks. "Yay!"

We all ran outside, sat down on the grass, and took off

our shoes. Then we each took off one sock and passed it to the next person—just like we had always done before each Kicks game, except this time we were swapping our everyday socks. Sarah, Zarine, and Grace saw us and came running over.

"Hey, don't leave us out!" Zarine said as they sat down on the grass with us.

"Next round!" I shouted, and we passed around our socks again, cracking up.

"You guys are so weird!"

It was Cody, who had showed up with Steven. Jessi jumped up and punched Cody in the arm.

"Weird? Did you say 'weird'?" she asked.

Cody laughed. "Okay, I take it back!"

Jessi had had the idea to ask the boys to help us with the clinic.

"Thanks for coming," I said. "Now I just hope some people show up."

"Well, I would say at least fifty," Steven said.

"How do you know that?" I asked him.

He pointed behind me. "Look!"

I turned around and saw that the parking lot of the community center had started to fill with minivans. Parents and kids were pouring out of the cars.

"Wow!" I said, starting to feel pumped up.

One of the minivans was the Marshmallow, and Mom walked up with Maisie.

"Mom!" I hugged her. "There are so many people here!"

"I asked the PTA to send an email to parents," Mom said. "Once people found out what you girls were doing, everybody wanted to support it."

"Thanks," I said, and then Dad walked up behind her, carrying some more cones. He had asked if he could help with the soccer clinic.

"If we raise enough funds, the school has said I can definitely coach," he said, "so this will be good practice."

"Wow, Dad, that's so cool," I said.

"It is!" Maisie said. "I'm so excited! Mom and I are going to help at the bake sale. I hope we sell a million cupcakes!"

I started to feel nervous. "I guess there's a lot riding on this."

"Don't worry. It looks like a good turnout already," Dad said, nodding to a line of kids and parents forming over by the side lawn. "What do you say we get things started?"

"Definitely!" I said, and Jessi and I jogged over to the side field with him, followed by Steven and Cody.

The morning went by in a flash. We had so many little kids show up! And they were all so cute! We had a lot of fun, but by one o'clock the crowds started to dwindle. Emma and the Tree Huggers had no more customers for their car wash.

I went inside and checked with Zoe.

"How are sales going?" I asked.

"Pretty good," Zoe said. "The necklaces are a big hit."

Emma walked up to us, taking a bite out of a white fluffy cupcake.

"Emma, that's the third time you've come in here for one!" Zoe said.

"I can't help it. They're delicious!" Emma replied. "Besides, they're for a good cause."

I looked around. A few people were walking around, but the morning crowd was definitely gone.

"I hope we made enough this morning to get the program going," I said. "It looks pretty dead now."

Zoe nodded. "Yeah. But at least we tried, you know. Maybe now that we did this fund-raiser, other people will try to help the soccer program too."

"I hope so," I said, but I was disappointed. I had been counting on the fair to save the soccer program so I could complete my hat trick!

"Let's get this party started!"

I knew that voice, of course. Once again Frida was making a dramatic entrance. We ran to greet her.

"Yay! You made it!" I said.

Frida smiled. "And I brought a friend."

She stepped away from the doorway to reveal a teenage boy with auburn hair and the most soulful brown eyes I had ever seen. Behind me Emma made a sound like a high-pitched fire whistle.

"Brady! Brady McCoy! Is here! He's actually here!" Emma squealed.

Brady smiled at her, totally not fazed by the fact that

she was having a major meltdown in front of him.

"You must be Emma," he said.

"Oh my gosh. He said my name!" Emma squealed again.

"Wow, it's nice to meet you," I said, shaking his hand. "I'm Devin, and this is Jessi and Zoe."

"It's so cool that you came here," Jessi said.

"Well, Frida talks about you guys all the time," he said. "Kicks, Kicks, Kicks. So I just had to meet you. Besides, this is a good cause."

"That's exactly what I just said!" Emma said.

By now some of the kids outside had started to come inside. Word that Brady was here was getting around fast.

"Uh-oh," I said. "Do you want to, like, hide somewhere?"

"I'm used to it," Brady said. "I don't mind signing a few autographs or something if it'll help out."

"Of course it will help!" Zoe said, excited. "Can we take a selfie with you and post it so people know that you're here?"

"Go for it!" Brady said cheerfully.

Zoe, Jessi, Emma, Frida, and I closed in around Brady, and Zoe snapped a selfie of all of us. After the flash we broke up, all of us giggling nervously. I wasn't a huge Brady fan like Emma, but he totally had this star quality about him. It was really exciting!

Emma ran to the craft table and pushed aside a display to make room for Brady.

"Here you go," she said. "You can sign autographs here."

"Brady McCoy is signing autographs!" somebody yelled

out, and now everybody outside was inside, hoping to get a chance to meet Brady.

Zoe brought a bunch of paper over from the craft table, along with some glitter pens. A little girl stepped up with her mom.

"What's your name?" Brady asked, flashing his amazing smile.

"Haley," said the girl in a shy, quiet voice.

"How do you spell that?" Brady asked.

"*H-A-L-E-Y*," the girl replied slowly.

Brady quickly wrote her a note and signed his name.

"Oh, thank you so much!" Haley's mom said.

Brady flashed that smile again. "You can thank me by making a donation to the Save the Soccer League Fund!"

On hearing that, Emma grabbed an empty box from under the craft table and held it out. The mom slipped a dollar into the box, and the next kid stepped up.

Zoe sidled up to me. "Okay, I can see why Emma is crazy about him now. He's a genius."

"And totally cute," I added.

"Cuter than Steven?" Zoe asked, with an evil look in her eye.

"Um, you know, it's—it's a different kind of cute," I stammered. "They're both cute!"

A few minutes later things got really crazy. Once people found out that Brady was at the soccer fair, they came right to the community center. Dad left the soccer clinic and came inside to help keep the line orderly. Jessi